Michael

A novella

By

Sandra Rowell

Dedicated

To

Michael

To whom I will be forever grateful

Published by
Cauliay Publishing & Distribution
PO Box 12076
Aberdeen
AB16 9AL
www.cauliaypublishing.com

First Edition
ISBN 978-0-9558992-0-1
Copyright © Sandra Rowell 2008
Cover design. © Cauliay Publishing
Cover picture by courtesy of Douglas Davidson

A CIP catalogue record for this book is available from the British Library.

Chapter 1

Michael James Brewer was born in the village of Hamilton, a sleepy village on the West Coast of England on 21st March 1985. It has perhaps 1,000 residents and to service them and see to their daily needs it has a post office, 3 pubs, several shops, a leisure centre, a doctor's surgery—which also doubles as a dentist—and a primary school. There is very little crime in the area so there is no need for a police station and unlike the bustling cities nowadays, there is no need to lock the door when you leave your home. Almost as though it is trapped in some kind of pre-war time warp; everyone in Hamilton knows everyone else and no-one would even think of entering another's property uninvited—unless it was to leave something rather than to take.

The village nestles in a valley surrounded by rolling hills and green fields stretching as far as the eye can see. In the early spring the air is filled with the song of nesting visitors, brought up from far off exotic places on the sweet breath of the warm Gulf-stream and in the summer the country paths are alive with foxglove and honeysuckle. An idyllic place to live really…or so one might think.

Michael is the eldest of two children born to Mary and David Brewer, the other being his little sister Madeleine who is 12 years old. To have an idea of the Brewer home one only has to think of the sleepy images of snow bound cottages on Victorian Christmas cards. Set in an acre of land it has everything except the horse drawn carriage. There are three bedrooms, a cosy living room, a neatly kept dining room, a real old country cottage kitchen with a quaint old fashioned cooking range, above it hangs a wooden clothes rack where Mary can hang the clothes in winter and hoist them up to dry above the stove. The bathroom is the only room in the house that has been thoroughly modernised. The outside of the property has several apple trees to the rear and, in the summertime, the front of the cottage is covered with a beautiful array of brightly coloured roses, they are David Brewer's pride and joy. To the left beneath the window sheltered by the cottage is a herb garden and beyond that is the vegetable patch. To the right a well manicured lawn. The cottage and its immediate garden are surrounded by a white picket fence.

The village primary school—built at the turn of the last century—looks over the village green where there is a pond complete with ducks and the occasional passing Canadian goose. Between four and eleven years of age Michael went to school there and by all accounts he was a very attentive student. His parents were aware from an early age that besides being a very thoughtful and imaginative young man, Michael had a very sensitive nature. Often he would bring home an injured hedgehog or a bird that had left the nest too early. He would devote himself to their care and nurse them back to health before setting them free again in their natural habitat. When the *surgery* was particularly busy— usually in the early spring when the birds were young and the hedgehogs still dopey from their long winter sleep—his mother would despair at the menagerie of beasts limping around the place like war weary casualties, but she knew that if anyone could nurse them back to health it was Michael; he had patience and love in his heart to spare—and she was deeply proud of that.

There is no secondary school in Hamilton, so the children are collected by bus and driven to the neighbouring village of Chiswick. Each day the same bus brings them home again. Many of Michael's friends lived in the village of Chiswick and as he grew older and of course when he wasn't tending his patients, this is where he tended to spend most of his free time.

Over the years Michael's love of animals developed to such a degree that on school holidays he could always be found working on the neighbouring farm with his father. The work on a farm is endless and to most people that would be a daunting thought but to a boy with the country in his blood it was paradise on earth. He loved nothing more than feeding the cows, rounding up the wayward sheep and feeding the ever-hungry pigs as they wallowed in the mud—it was because of their lifestyle that he was perhaps not so keen on cleaning out the pig stys. Dad would tease him tell him it was: "Just the fragrances of nature," when he complained of the smells. Horses were Michael's real passion; he loved everything about them—including the smell. Occasionally old Dawson would let him ride on the back of the horse as it pulled the cart to market and for him it was the highlight of his day. He might only have been riding on the friendly old cob taking the cart full of fresh milk, eggs and other farm produce to the market, but in his mind he was sitting proud like a Royal Horse Guard riding gallantly down the Mall in front of ten thousand cheering sight-seers.

Market day was Saturday. Villagers from all the neighbouring villages would come to buy and sell. It was Michael's job to look after the stall with the home made jams, chutneys and all other home made produce.

He loved every minute of market day the buzz and the cheery banter from farmer's wives and the meetings now and then with some friends of his own age from school. Market day was a long day and Michael would often go home at night exhausted, but wonderfully content.

At the age of 16, Michael left school and went to work on the farm full time and before long with the combination of fine food, fresh air and hard graft his body was forged into that of a strapping young man. By the age of 19, he was simply an Adonis. His rugged, film star looks were complimented by his big broad shoulders. His muscles covered with a golden brown skin rippled in the heat of the summer sunshine as he toiled away in the fields. His physique, coupled with his blonde hair and deep blue eyes made Michael a favourite of all the young women in the village. There was never a shortage of girls wanting to be seen with him, although he did not have a regular girlfriend as yet.

One summer's evening at the end of the week Michael had just finished work. He arrived home from a hard day in the fields. Madeleine had seen him walking up the garden path and decided to surprise him. As he walked through the door she jumped out from her hiding place and into his half expectant arms. Michael loved his little sister and he knew all of her little surprises. He had been 8 years old when she was born so at first he was not too thrilled about having a crying machine around the place but as she grew older he came to love her more than anything. He was always protective of her and all the boys in her class knew that her pigtails were *definitely* out of bounds.

He laughed as she pretended to box him and they ended up in a wrestling match on the floor. Soon they were rolling all over the place and laughing until their faces ached, their playful antics were only interrupted when their mother called them to the table.

After tea, Michael decided that—as the weather had suddenly turned bad—he was going to stay in and play games with Madeleine to pass the night away: the format of the evening had more or less already been set by her earlier ambush.

By 11 o'clock, Madeleine was tired and it was only the presence of Michael that was forcing her to keep her weary eyes open. It was only when her mother ordered her to bed that she gave in to the call of sleep and trudged upstairs to bed. She whispered a sleepy, "Goodnight," to everyone and in a final play of giddiness she gave Michael a playful thump on his back. He took his cue as usual and chased up the stairs after her.

Seven o'clock on a Saturday morning, and the sun outside was already climbing high into the sky. A ray of sunshine sliced through the gap in the curtains like a laser-beam as Michael awoke and stretched. He lay in his bed looking at the ceiling with his hands clasped behind his head and a smile on his handsome young face. He was thinking about the day ahead. The birds were singing in their frantic morning chorus and, with the fresh smells of another beautiful day wafting in through the open window, this promised to be a wonderful weekend. He did not work on Saturday so there was no need to hurry. He lifted his fingers into the ray of sunlight knowing that he could take as much time as he wanted to do exactly what he liked.

Madeleine knocked on his door and peeped into his room asking to come in. Michael didn't answer; he just playfully made a face at her as if he were expecting another onslaught. She got the message and instead of an all-out assault she quietly sat on the edge of his bed. They chatted away about her week at school and what she and her friends had been up to. Michael and his parents had always instilled into Madeleine the need for a good education. She was a good, industrious student and Michael was always ready to listen to her and give her advice if she asked for it. This morning, she had a sad look on her face. Michael asked her what was wrong. She paused and thought for a moment before asking Michael if he was alright.

"Why do you ask that, Maddy?" he smiled.

"I don't know exactly," she said, "I just have a funny feeling that something is going to happen today; something bad."

Michael sat up and held his powerful hand out towards her. She moved in closer and he put his arm around her shoulder and told her not to worry.

"What could possibly happen to us? We have great parents, I have a beautiful little sister, and you have a fabulous—and gorgeous big brother. So what more do we need?" he whispered as he brushed her hair from her face.

Madeleine's face looked angelic as the ray of light lit up her golden hair: "I don't know Michael; I just have a strange feeling in my stomach, a feeling that something is not right."

Despite Michael's brotherly assurances Madeleine would know by the end of the day that her strange feelings were not without foundation.

By 8am, Michael was showered and dressed and to his knowledge his little sister had had her mind put at ease. He sat at the kitchen table with the rest of the family and ate a hearty breakfast of bacon, eggs, sausages and beans topped off with a big steaming mug of hot tea—a breakfast fit for any farmhand. After breakfast he told his parents that he would be out for the rest of the day; then as he playfully kissed Madeleine on the head he reminded his mum that he would be home in time for supper.

Saturday was the day he spent with his friends and this Saturday was going to be no different than any other. Every weekend Michael would head off to Chiswick to meet up with his friends. Their routine seldom varied; meeting in the village square, a few drinks and a meal in the local pub, a bit of fun with some of the local girls and plenty of laughter. A far cry from the things they used to do as children.

Michael had many endearing qualities, but the one slight chink in his otherwise pristine nature was that he was extremely wary of people he did not know and Michael would take his time in getting to know someone he had met for the first time. Although he had an obvious outgoing zest for life according to the people who were close to him, he could appear distant and even morose to someone new. He was a child that any parent would be proud of, but along with every growing boy there is some level of excusable waywardness and Michael was no different in that sense. He got into his fair share of trouble for breaking windows whilst playing football or cricket with his pals in the streets of Chiswick, and like his friends he would run away filled with the childish excitement of his misdemeanour. Of course, when the local bobby tracked down the culprit and his parents subsequently found out what he had done, he was made to pay for the windows and punished accordingly, but having said that he was always forgiven to a fair degree by the fact that there was nowhere really for the young to play in a quiet little village. The old folk had their bowling green and there was a small park area where mothers could sit and watch their toddlers on the swings but there was nothing at all for the teenagers. The aging village council always managed to resist pressure from young parents to *destroy the village's unspoilt beauty in favour of a concrete playground or, Heaven forbid a sports field that would 'Attract all forms of low life' in the dead of night.* The consequence of that archaic outlook was football in the street and of course the odd broken window. Michael's other—less expensive pastime—was climbing trees. Often he would climb to the top of the tallest tree just to sit and watch the world go by in miniature.

As he grew up, Michael changed in many ways. Tree-climbing, football, his beloved cricket bat and his toys were put away to be replaced with other things like girls, sport and going to the pub. Through all of his adolescent changes the one constant in his life was his unquenchable sense of fun.

By the time Michael was twenty, he was tall and strong and incredibly handsome, in short, his parents were very proud of him. He was a young man who enjoyed life to the full and was loved by all who knew him. I say Michael was a young man… because Michael is dead. Rather than achieving his lifetime's ambitions and fulfilling the dreams of his doting parents he has become just another statistic in the crime records of an already over-stretched police force; another, in the long list of unsolved murders in the whole of the West of

11

England.   But, the story does not end there…because Michael had no intentions of staying dead.

Chapter 2

Donald Wiseman had been born into a family that showed him no love or affection. He was conceived as a result of the drunken rape of his mother by his father and he was delivered into this world on 20th August 1975. It had been a bright and warm summer's day but there was no sunshine in his mother's face when she was handed her newborn son. Instead there was a look of pity. She knew in her broken heart that this helpless little boy was going to have a hard life; it was perhaps just as well that this baby had not been born a girl.

Donald's parents were—to all intents—a couple who put their own lives above all else and they did so for their own particular, and very different reasons…that was until baby Donald came along. At first Donald's mother, Sylvia, did try to be a good mother to her son but she was thwarted every step of the way by her domineering husband, so much so that in the end she gave up trying to do what was right for her son to concentrate wholly on her own survival. Despite the constant fights that Donald had been forced to witness since his birth he always knew deep down that his mother loved him.

Under such strained circumstances it was no surprise that the young Donald grew to be an introverted youth who frequently played truant from school; in fact, he so rarely attended lessons that it was a wonder he ever learned to read and write at all. Yet, and despite his short-comings, he was by no means without natural intelligence—quite the opposite in fact.

Education of their son did not seem to be of importance to his warring parents and as long as he kept out of their way they did not seem to care where he was, whom he was with, or what he did. And so it was that Donald was left to fend for himself and he learned quickly to live by his wits, for, like his mother, he too understood that his ultimate destiny rested firmly in his own hands.

Donald's father—Jack—was well known in the village and outlying district for his hard drinking and with it more often than not came bouts of unpredictable violence; young Donald was usually his victim. If his mother tried to intervene, he turned his fists on her so she usually kept out of the way and would sit with her hands covering her ears to block out her son's pitiful cries.

At the age of ten, Donald suffered a particularly vicious beating from his father for no other reason than he just happened to be sitting on *his* chair when he came home from another marathon drinking binge. Without so much as a word his fist crashed into the side of his son's face knocking him, semi-conscious to the floor. As he tried to lift his body, his father's boot drove into his ribs so hard that he felt as though his lungs would burst. Donald endured the beating until his drunken father stumbled into the kitchen to take another beer from the fridge.

Unbeknown to his father Donald had built himself a little hideaway under the front porch, and it was to this place that he dragged his battered body on his hands and knees with tears of pain and confusion streaming down his battered face. From there, he could see everything that was happening inside the house. He watched as his mother came silently into the kitchen and put his father's supper on the table. He watched as his father picked up the plate and flung it against the wall in a fit of rage. He watched as his mother tried to clean up the mess. He watched as she asked why he had done it and he watched as his father clenched his fists and battered his wife to the floor. Her beating did not end with her unconsciousness; he kicked her in the face until the blood ran from her shattered mouth and spilled onto the linoleum covered floor. Donald shivered helplessly; all he could do was wait in the cold silence until his father went to bed to *sleep it off* before he could sneak out to comfort his mother. The scene unfolding before his eyes was not new or rare. It had happened to him on many occasions, but watching as his mother was being beaten almost to death was the straw that broke the camel's back…something in his mind snapped.

Donald usually waited until he knew for certain that his father was well out of the way before he dare venture from his secret refuge, but on this day he crawled out to tend to his mother as his father's heavy footsteps faded into silence. He cradled his mother's battered head in the crook of his arm as he gently brushed her blood matted hair from her face. Then—without knowing how he had gotten there—he suddenly became aware that he was standing at the kitchen door looking into the living room at his father. He saw the evil face of his father as he sat in an armchair drinking his beer as if he had just come in from a hard day's work. He held the can of beer up as if to say "Cheers" and he smiled an evil grin. Donald looked at his father and it took all of his inner strength to stop himself from killing him there and then. Luckily, common sense and his natural instinct for survival kicked in; he knew that he was too weak from his beating and that his father would easily overpower him. Instead he looked at his father and vowed that one day soon he would end those beatings once and for all… and until that day he would bide his time.

Chapter 3

Over the following weeks as he and his mother slowly recovered, he did all he could to steer clear of his father. During that time Donald noticed a change in his mother. She had become morose and uncommunicative; her actions were like those of a zombie, slow and robotic. She was forgetful and distant and the light in her eyes that was always subdued yet still evident was now just a grey ember in cold hearth. It was painfully obvious to Donald that the last beating had done more than just physical damage.

One day Donald came home to find his mother slumped in the armchair in the living room; it was mid-afternoon and he immediately feared the worst. He knew that she would never have dared to take a nap with chores still to be done. He let his coat drop to the floor and rushed over to his mother, she was still breathing, but she was clearly in a coma. He put his hands under her body to carry her upstairs to bed; it was only when he got to his feet that he realised that his mother's frail body had almost wasted away to nothing, she was little more than a rag-doll in his arms. He carried her easily through the house and laid her gently on her bed before he called for the doctor. He knew that he would risk taking a terrible beating by not contacting his father first, but he also knew that his father would not have called for the doctor because his guilt would have stopped him.

That was to be the last day of her life on this earth and thankfully Donald was with her at the end. The subsequent coroner's report said that she died of massive organ failure brought on by severe malnutrition and the fact that there was food in the house pointed towards some kind of un-diagnosed mental illness leading up to her death. Throughout the hearing Jack played the grieving husband with a stunning performance and Donald sat in silence as the final verdict was read out. He could have told the hearing the truth behind his mother's death, but—and despite his youth—he knew that any sentence handed out would never be enough to pay for the crime his father had committed. He had already made one vow; that he was going to stop the beatings. In that courtroom he made another vow; that he would avenge his mother's murder before the year was out.

Six months after her death Donald's father was still keeping up his performance as the grieving widower and he milked the misplaced kindness of his neighbours to the full. Yet in the privacy of his own home, safe behind closed doors he was still the same brute to his son that he had always been. Donald was forced to take on the role of house-keeper to his father and he did so with stoical resolution…because he had a plan.

Whenever it was safe to do so Donald would go to his secret den beneath the house. Since his mother's death he had turned it into a shrine to her memory and he would sit talking to her as if she were still by his side. Late one afternoon after his father had left the house Donald waited until he was certain that he would be gone for the evening, it was Friday and his father was unlikely to return until the early hours of Saturday morning. He crept out of the house and within minutes he slipped silently into his hideaway. He sat in the darkness and waited for his eyes to become accustomed to it. To light a lamp was out of the question, the glow would be seen from a mile away so as usual his routine was to sit and recite the vow he had made to avenge his mother's death. That was how he always opened his conversations with his dead mother. As he began to speak he sensed an uneasiness about him; he felt that there was something wrong, something different about the place. He turned his ear to the eerie silence to perhaps find a clue to the source of his growing anxiety. A flood of swirling thoughts burst into his mind and his heart pounded like thunder in his chest. Was that a footfall in the distance? Was his father returning home unexpectedly? How could he get back into the house without his father seeing him? He clenched his fists to his ears to silence the thoughts, he needed to think clearly. He forced himself to sit still and analyse what was real and what was in his imagination. Slowly the myriad of stinging thoughts subsided and once again silence filled the growing gloom around him. He told himself that the noise he heard was probably a stray dog nuzzling through the dustbins for scraps. Satisfied that he was safe, he spoke once again to his mother: "Mother I saw what he did to you, I watched him punch you and kick you until you died. I wanted to help you but I was too small. I wanted to tell the people in that courtroom that you were killed by that pig that is my father, but I couldn't do it. I couldn't do it because I am going to kill him myself."

The moment the words left his mouth a fist flew out of the darkness and thundered into the side of his face and he heard his father's rasping voice as he collapsed to the ground. His father put his massive hands around his son's neck and began to squeeze the life from him. "You are not going to kill anyone you pathetic little bastard. You are worse than the miserable whore who gave birth to you and ruined my life. I could have been somebody in this town if I didn't have you two hanging round my neck like chains. Well now I'm going to break free of you both, you can die here with your bitch of a mother."

Donald's father had found the shrine days earlier and he had set a trap to find out what his son was up to. That evening instead of going to the local bar to drink himself to oblivion, he had left the house and doubled back to lay in wait. He listened as Donald swore to avenge his mother's death when he grew up. The venom in his son's voice made him realize that his son would kill him one day, so to him—in his demented rage—it was a simple matter of kill or be killed.

As his fingers tightened around his son's throat he began to hatch an evil plan. He could kill his son and set fire to the house to destroy any evidence. He still had time to go to the bar and that would give him a perfect alibi. Once again he would be the poor grieving father who had lost everything. He could still be the man he had always planned to be. As the plan grew in his mind the life of his son ebbed away in his hands and he let his limp body fall to the ground. He would have to move fast if his alibi was to work. He crawled from beneath the house and went into the living room. He tore up some newspaper and stuffed it behind the cushions on the worn out sofa, then he pushed the table over to the window and set fire to the curtains, he lit the paper on the sofa and waited a few moments until he was certain that the fire had taken hold. On his way out he opened the gas tap on the cooker. Within minutes he was in the bar enjoying a friendly beer and in his house the fire raged above the body of his dead son...or so he thought.

The fire did take hold of the house and the gas exploding did have the desired effect, it ripped the house apart, but it also had another unexpected effect. Donald's eyes began to twitch and the inferno raging above him seemed somehow to draw the life back into him. He retched in the darkness of his would-be tomb and suddenly his lungs filled with air. Donald's father had failed to strangle the life out of him, instead his body had gone into shut-down, the same kind of shut-down that has seen children revived after spending half an hour trapped under the ice of a frozen lake. The explosion above him had shaken his body back into recovery mode. Not fully aware of where he was or what was happening, he lay still on the ground. Moments later he heard voices calling his name. Fortunately his neighbours had heard the blast and dashed over to help. His throat was too badly damaged to call out and his face ached from the blow his father had struck, but he had the determination to survive and the strength to crawl out. As the sirens echoed in the distance through the darkness of the night Donald was spotted by a neighbour as he staggered from beneath the house and fell into her arms. His back was burned from the falling debris above him but apart from that and of course the beating from his father, he was relatively unscathed. Once out of harm's way the neighbour wrapped her coat around him and waited for the arrival of the ambulance. The fire services were the first on the scene and they soon had the blaze under control. Donald managed an inward smile as he was helped into the ambulance, because he knew that his prison was gone forever and his plans for his father were still—like him—very much alive.

Chapter 4

News of the fire soon spread to the bar where Donald's father was drinking with his friends and again he played the part of a man in emotional turmoil; he collapsed when he heard that it was his house that was on fire and he raged uncontrollably when his friends tried to reassure him that his 'poor boy' might not have perished in the flames. Jack pushed them away when he had apparently regained his strength and some semblance of composure. "He must be dead," he cried, "When I left him he was sleeping like a baby. Oh my son, my poor son, what have I done to him? It should have been me in those flames." Right at the end of his command performance two police officers entered the bar looking for him. "Are you Mr Jack Wiseman?" one of them asked. Jack looked at them and put his hands together as if in prayer. "You have come to tell me that my son is dead haven't you," he sobbed, "I just know it."

"Now calm down sir, we don't have any information yet, we have been asked to take you over to the hospital," the second officer said. Jacks mind suddenly went into overdrive...*Hospital, why hospital?* He walked with them as they quickly escorted him to their waiting car. Meanwhile over at the hospital young Donald was busy planning a performance of his own. Despite his pain and the horrendous ordeal he had been through he managed to collect his thoughts and put them together in a way that would ensure his long-term survival. He made up his mind that he would pretend to have lost his memory completely; he would not remember the fire, the beatings, his bullying father…nothing. If he could pull it off and convince his father that he had no recollection of events, then his father would have no reason to try to kill him again. He knew that he would be taking a massive chance but he had already decided that it was that, or die. He was not to know it at the time but providence was about to step in unexpectedly and help him to bring his plan to a glorious conclusion.

Donald lay on the hospital bed as a steady stream of medical staff filed in to look at him. In between tending to his injuries they asked him questions; all Donald did was beg to see his father. Outside the hospital, the police car screeched to a halt and the two officers went with him into casualty, through the melee of medical staff and nurses someone stepped forward and offered to take them to Donald's bedside. His father didn't know what to expect when the curtains were drawn to one side to allow him into the cubicle, one thing though is for certain, that he could never have prepared himself for what happened next. The moment Donald saw his father he leaped from the bed and flung himself into his father's arms. "Daddy, please take me home," he cried. His father was taken completely by surprise and all he could do was sink to his knees and hold onto his son as if his life depended on it. He was crying and shaking, but this time it was no act, he was confused and didn't know what else to do. His son should have been dead and burned to a cinder; not two hours earlier he thought he had strangled the life out of his son and yet here he was clinging to him as though, they were inseparable…it didn't make sense. It was only when the doctor appeared that things started to drop into place. "My staff have work to do sir, your son has multiple abrasions and a very nasty burn on his back, I can escort you to a waiting room and fix you up with a coffee whilst we see what needs to be done," the doctor said.

Jack looked at Donald and looked at the two police officers before he asked: "Will he be alright?"

The doctor led Donald's father out of earshot of his son and said: "He is in quite considerable distress but his condition is not life threatening, apart from the nasty burn he has some bruising on his neck, probably from trying to squeeze out through a gap that was too small. I am more concerned though by the blow to the head he seems to have suffered; it seems to have left him with memory loss. He says he can't remember anything about the fire or how he arrived here."

Jack seized the opportunity to resume his acting role, in an instant he was once again the doting father and the grieving widower. "He has never been quite the same since his poor mother died," he said as he hung his head. One of the police officers put a supportive hand on his shoulder and patted him reassuringly. "Why don't you come through and have a coffee whilst we wait for some news?"

"That would be a good idea," the doctor added.

The police officers sat with Donald's father as they waited for Donald to be fully examined. "Have you anywhere to stay tonight?" one of the officers asked.

Jack shrugged his shoulders: "The only thing I care about right now is my little boy," he said. The rest of the wait was more or less spent in total silence.

Back in the cubicle Donald was being tended to as he tried to evaluate the success of his plan so far. It seemed to be working well in as far as the doctor was convinced of his memory loss. He knew that his father would be a harder nut to crack but he also knew that he had no other choice but to try to see it through.

An hour or so passed and what was to be the first of a very fortunate series of events for Donald took place. The neighbour who had helped Donald at the scene of the blaze arrived at the hospital and offered to take Jack and his son in until they could find an alternative place to live. Jack was in no position to refuse even though it would mean that he would have to be on his best behaviour at all times. Not long after the neighbour arrived the doctor appeared to tell Jack that Donald would be kept in hospital overnight for precautionary observation and if he felt strong enough to leave in the morning, then he could take his son home. Jack asked if he could see his son again and the doctor led him through. Donald's poor face lit up again at the sight of his father and Jack responded by cradling his son's outstretched hand in his.

"The doctor says you will have to stay in overnight," Jack said in a voice filled with a well thought out mixture of hope and anguish. Donald responded in an equally false yet equally convincing fashion.

"I want to go home with you daddy, I'm scared here," he said, before turning to the doctor and pleading for his father to be allowed to stay.

The doctor shook his head: "I'm afraid that won't be possible young man, you need absolute rest and don't forget that your father has been through a lot too this evening. He has many things to do before we can allow you to return home."

"That's right, son," his father said, "You sleep now whilst I find us a place to stay for when you are allowed home."

Donald lay back and smiled: "Promise me that you will be back first thing in the morning."

"I promise," Jack said, as he turned to leave the room. A moment or two later he was back in the waiting room and he was not happy with what he found.

Back in the waiting room the kindly neighbour was sitting next to the police officers as one of them spoke and the other one took notes. The conversation stopped abruptly giving Jack the distinct impression that it was he that was being spoken of and that it was probably not in such a flattering light. He decided that attack was the best form of defence. "Is there something wrong officer?" he asked.

"We need to talk to you sir about one or two things but they can wait until morning, you have had a rather traumatic evening sir. Could you pop into the station in Chiswick sometime tomorrow?" the officer with the notebook asked.

"I have a lot to do tomorrow, can't you ask your questions now?" he said trying to control his irritation.

The officer blew out his cheeks and sighed: "I don't want this to sound bad, but under the circumstances I'm afraid that it might not be possible to put it any other way."

"I'm a man of the world officer, I know you have to ask difficult questions, but I have nothing to hide." Jack said, continuing and building on his air of innocence.

"Then I will ask you bluntly sir, why did you leave your son in the house on his own?"

"Have I broken any laws?" Jack asked.

"Now steady on sir, no one has suggested that, I am merely asking a question that someone is bound to ask sooner or later. Look, it's late and you have had a very trying day, I really do think it will be better to talk about this after you have had some rest."

"Don't patronise me officer, you are not the one without a home and you are not the one with a son in hospital. Now, have I done anything against the law?"

"Alright sir, I apologise, I didn't mean to sound patronizing. As far as I know there is no legal age at which a child can or can not be left alone. However, it is an offence to leave a child at home alone when doing so would put the child at risk. Now, the Social Services will need a report from me so that they can decide if by you leaving your child alone—and in the light of what happened—any offence was committed."

Jack seemed to calm down and he stood in silence for a few moments before he answered. He thought that his policy of attack was perhaps losing him some sympathy; he needed to buy himself some thinking time. "Yes officer, I see where you are coming from. Donald was safely tucked up in bed and I decided that it would be alright to slip out for the last half hour for a drink or two."

"That's just what I thought," the policeman said, "So, I'll put that in my report and we will leave it there for now, if we need you again where can we contact you?"

The kindly neighbour once again offered Jack a bed until he found an alternative. She gave the police her address and Jack agreed to take advantage of her kindness. The policeman offered Jack and his neighbour a lift home and that put an end to the day's events.

The following day Donald was discharged from hospital into the care of his father and both arrived back at their neighbour's house to find that she had hung a sheet above the front door which read: 'Welcome home to a very brave boy'

Jack and Donald had not been at their neighbour's house for two days before they had a call from a smartly dressed couple from the child welfare services. They had obviously read the police report and decided to follow it up. Jack answered their questions very feasibly but he could sense that they were spoiling for the case to go before the local magistrate. His reputation as being not quite the doting father as he would have liked them to think had been leaked to the Social Services and they had done some digging around into his past and in particular, his drinking habits. After an hour or so of tough questioning they closed their notebook and told Jack that they would be in touch. Jack knew that the interpretation of that was that they would indeed be taking him to court.

Chapter 5

When Jack had left school years earlier he had served his time as an apprentice butcher but when he was fully qualified he decided to find work at the local slaughterhouse rather than work at the retail end of things. After a number of years the slaughterhouse closed down and he found work with a local butcher who was nearing retirement age. In the past the butcher had asked Jack if he wanted to buy him out when his retirement was imminent but until then Jack had always declined. Now with his future uncertain and with his mind in overdrive with the possibility of a court conviction hanging over him he thought that perhaps the money from the insurance on the house would be enough to buy the business and give himself the standing in society that would show the community that he had changed his former ways and that he was intent on building a steady future for himself and his son. He didn't waste any time in putting his plan into action and once again the gods seemed to be smiling down on him. His old boss readily agreed to sell him the shop and the living accommodation above it; that deal alone solved one immediate issue although he would have to wait six months until he could officially take over the house. Once again his neighbour offered to accommodate him and his son until the house was free to move into. Jack had indeed landed on his feet, Donald was making a good recovery thanks mainly to the loving care of the neighbour, although it was becoming increasingly obvious—and once again in Jack's favour—that Donald would never regain his memory of what happened on that fateful night or indeed in the years leading up to it.

By the time of the court hearing everything was cemented in place.

The Social Services put forward a very forceful case that Donald should be made a ward of court for his safety. In return Jack put forward a defence of equal force and in the final summing up it was Donald's contribution to proceedings which tipped the balance in his father's favour. The judge took the unusual step of asking Donald how he would feel about being separated from his father. It was during that courtroom performance that Donald outshone the master...his father when it came to acting.

"Sir," he began, "Mrs Fairchild our neighbour has been looking after my father and I for the past few months and if she is allowed to carry on looking after us so that my father can go to work then everything will be just like it was when mummy was here with us."

His performance was stunning and there was not a dry eye in the courtroom. The judge asked Mrs Fairchild if she did indeed intend to play a major part in his up-bringing for the foreseeable future and she of course agreed. And so the case of Donald's childhood was resolved in that courtroom. His father would build up his business and the bringing up of Donald would be done between Jack and the delightful Mrs Fairchild. The Social services would still be involved with three monthly visits but to all intents and purposes Donald's future was secure...the first part of his plan had gone according to plan beautifully.

Chapter 6

In the years that followed Donald grew into a fine young man. His physical scars healed and faded into insignificance with every passing day, but the scars of his mother's death burned like a branding iron into his heart with every passing day. And it was in his heart that he re-built the shrine to his mother that had been destroyed so many years before. To a watching world Jack and his father were as close as any father and son but every night before he put his head down to sleep he told his mother that one day her lonesome death would be spectacularly avenged.

When Donald reached the age of leaving school there was only ever going to be one place that he was going to work and that of course was alongside his devoted father. In the interim years Jack had put his past behind him and his business had flourished. So, on the day Donald left school he was officially apprenticed to his own father and Jack took on the role of teaching his son everything he knew about the age-old craftsmanship of butchery. Donald was an eager apprentice and before long he was going about his duties like a skilled professional. He could bone a side of beef with the finesse of a surgeon and his work with the cleaver was nothing short of dynamic, he could slice through a rack of cutlets with millimetre precision. On his eighteenth birthday Jack took him out to the front of the shop and told him to close his eyes. When he opened them he saw his father and Mrs Fairchild holding a bottle of champagne and above the shop window was written the words 'Wiseman & Son Master Butchers'. Donald's face broke into a wonderful smile as he ran to embrace the couple who had been his whole life for the past eight years. He hugged them both as the champagne cork popped into the air, but amidst the laughter and the fondness Donald smiled an inward smile of deep satisfaction because he knew that his plan had taken another massive leap towards its ultimate conclusion. Donald knew that his father had been totally disarmed…now it was just a matter of time and opportunity. Just as the early morning birthday surprise was drawing to a close Donald had another surprise waiting for him. His father ducked back inside the shop and emerged moments later with a fine pair of fishing rods.

"Happy birthday son," he smiled as he handed them to Donald.

Donald looked at them in admiration, "Thanks dad, they're beautiful."

"Only the best for you my son, and tomorrow we will put them to good use. The two of us are going on a fishing trip, two men together," Jack smiled.

"That will be fantastic dad," Donald said, "I really can't wait."

Early the following morning just as the sun was about to break in the eastern sky Donald awoke to the sound of birds singing in the trees. He went downstairs to find his father already up and dressed. A pan full of sausages was already sizzling on the stove and the fishing rods were packed up ready to move out when the sun was fully up.

"You are up early dad," Donald said sleepily.

"I have waited all my life for today son, the day when I could spend some time with my boy when he had come of age. I know life hasn't always been easy for you, but on a day like this, there isn't a moment to lose, its days like this that makes life worth living. Come on, tuck in and let's hit the road and blood our new rods," Jack smiled.

Donald looked at his father and nodded: "We have each other now, partners in everything and that makes up for the hard things in life."

Father and son sat at the table and shared a hearty meal. Then, as Jack loaded up the car with fishing tackle, Donald prepared a picnic hamper for them both. Before long they were heading out through picturesque country lanes towards their destination and neither man seemed to have a care in the world. At a secluded spot about twelve miles out in the middle of nowhere the car rolled to a halt. They took the gear and walked down to the river and found a nice peaceful spot where they set up their rods. Donald poured them a coffee from the flasks he had brought and they sat and talked. Before too long, they were laughing and talking like the best of friends. The hours passed in a glorious air of bonding and friendship and every so often Jack gave an audible sigh of sheer contentment.

By early evening as the sun was beginning to dip low in the sky they were tired but happy although not one fish had been caught. The Rods had not been 'Bloodied' but the day had been a success on a far more important level so far as Jack was concerned and now it was time for them to pack up and head home. As they were packing up Jack suddenly did something very strange, he turned to Donald and said: "I'm really very sorry for not being the kind of father you needed when you were growing up Donald. My only excuse is that I had no idea what being a father actually meant. Now you are a full grown man, I hope it's not too late for me to make amends for all those lost years, you know, the forgotten years; the years before the fire. Can you ever forgive me son?"

His father's words hit Donald like a runaway train because he knew that his father had deliberately lowered his defences so that he could test him and catch him off guard. His anger boiled inside him but he had learned to deal with it over the years and in a way he felt admiration for the level of his father's deceit and callousness. *This bastard still doesn't know if I remember anything.* The only way to respond was in kind and Donald too had a trick or two of his own. Donald laid his fishing tackle back on the ground and slowly turned to face his father and said: "Dad, the only life I have ever known is the life we have had since that fire. I have tried to remember things before then but there is only sleep. I know I must have had a mother and I know that you must miss her terribly but nothing either one of us does will bring her back. There is no future in the past so I think it best if we just put it to bed and get on with the rest of our lives, don't you?" Jack breathed a sigh of relief, outwardly because his son had showed tremendous maturity but inwardly because he knew that he was finally in the clear. "Thank you son. Somehow I am going to make it up to you even if it takes the rest of my life I'm going to make sure we stay friends." Jack walked up to his son, stopped for a few moments with his head bowed then he wrapped his arms around Donald and Donald returned the gesture. They stayed that way for a moment or two and, as they parted, Donald noticed tears running down his father's face. Jack was a happy man. At last he had gained his son's forgiveness and his unconditional affection, something he knew full well he did not deserve. With their arms around each other's shoulders, they walked slowly back to the waiting car. Jack drove home with a smile on his face that showed that the world was a marvellous place to live.

Back at home he prepared supper for them both and, as they ate and drank a few beers, they talked about other things they could do together. The two men sat until at last, Jack declared himself very tired and feeling rather drunk he decided it was time for bed. He made his weary way to the stairs after saying to Donald: "Goodnight son, see you in the morning."

Donald smiled and waved, "Goodnight dad."

Donald listened as his father began to walk up the stairs and a coldness shadowed his heart. The last time he had listened to his father's footsteps was on the night of the fire…the only difference being that on this night Donald was the one who had set the trap. Jack did not realise he felt so tired and drunk because Donald had spiked his beer. Jack had gone no further than five steps up the staircase when his head began to swim. After a moment or two Donald heard a loud thump. Very slowly he got out of his chair and went to the kitchen door. There was his father lying flat on the floor, face down at the foot of the staircase. Donald didn't give his actions a moment's thought, he didn't have to, he had run that moment through his mind ten thousand times. He knelt on his father's back and strangled him as he lay unconscious. He strangled him in exactly the same way as his father had tried to strangle him all those years before and what was more…he knew exactly what he was going to do with his father's body.

Donald lifted his father's body and took it out to the car before he drove to the butcher's shop. It was late on Sunday night and the village was peacefully asleep, the only thing moving was an old hedgehog and a stray tom cat and neither of them would testify to anything. He was confident he would not be observed carrying the body into the shop but still, erring on the side of caution, he carried it in through the back doors. He quickly stripped the body of all its clothes and the only thing verging on emotion was how it felt strange seeing his father naked for the first and last time in his life. Donald took out his cleaver and, after making sure it was extra sharp, he began to cut up the body. First of all, he chopped off the head, saying as he did so: "Now Donald, you have to lift the cleaver up high and make sure you bring it down hard so there is a clean break." *No broken bits of bone for Mister Smith to complain about.* Next he cut off the arms and legs saying as he did so: "Be careful when you use the saw. You have to saw through the ball joint so as not to damage the meat." As he began to feed his father's limbs through the mincing machine he said out loud: "Be careful with this machine otherwise you will take off your own hand." He continued in this way until the last of the body had gone through the machine and there was not a single trace that he had ever existed…at last his mother's murder had been avenged.

With the stripped bones crushed and added to the bones for collection Donald's work was done for the night and he calmly made his way home to bed.

Chapter 7

Because he had spent so many years under the protection of Mrs Fairchild and of course under the constant glare of the Social Services, the sheltered Donald had missed out on some of the normal activities of the young. He had never been encouraged to enjoy the company of friends his own age and of course that included members of the opposite sex. In short he rarely had the chance to lead what you or I would classify as a normal life. As a consequence of this, he grew to be quite a guarded, almost jealous young man with a suspicion of all people around him and in particular the young. Probably because he felt excluded and that they had something that he had missed out on. Growing up in the classroom he had always been one of those quiet children who seem to drift through school without bringing attention upon themselves. He was neither loud nor sporty nor particularly academic, he was however just the sort of candidate to slip under the radar of any hard-pressed teacher. He did what was required of him and no more, the other kids thought he was 'odd' but apart from that he was more or less left alone.

By the time of his eighteenth birthday he stood at about 5'6" height and his brown hair and Spanish eyes gave him a kind of smouldering Latino look. The most striking feature he had was his sparkling white teeth. He was always a very clean, tidy young man who rarely spoke to anyone. In the shop he was always polite to the customers because his father had instilled that businessman aspect of politeness into him. So, when he had to deal with the public he was careful to do it with precision and economy. He had become as un-noticeable in his working life as he had in his schooldays, and that suited him just fine. It wasn't until he reported his father's disappearance that he discovered just how un-noticeable he really was.

Donald waited until the following Tuesday morning before he thought about going to the police station to tell them that his father had gone missing. His original plan had been to march into the station in Chiswick and confess the whole thing, after all his vow to his mother had been fulfilled and his life's work lay on the mincing tray in the freezer. But on reflection he thought he would have some fun and see how long it would take them to discover where his father actually was after he had reported him missing. The first person Donald saw at the police station was the duty desk sergeant.

"Yes Donald, what can I do for you?" he asked cheerfully.

"Well, my father went out somewhere on Sunday evening after we returned from a fishing trip for my birthday. I thought he was nipping out to collect a surprise present for me so I didn't ask where he was going. The thing is, he hasn't been back since and I haven't heard from him either, I'm getting worried."

"Have you any idea where he might be?" the sergeant asked.

"I have tried Mrs Fairchild's house and he isn't there and that's the only place I can think of."

"Right, I see," the sergeant said looking bemused, "I know we can't list him as officially missing until he had been gone for a full 48 hours, so you get yourself off home and see if he turns up, if he is still missing in the morning we can move things on a stage. Listen, don't worry, he's a big lad and he can look after himself, he's bound to turn up at home when he's hungry. He's probably got himself embroiled in a card game."

Donald did as he was told and went home. The following morning he opened the shop and after he rang the police he started to bag up the mince and put it out on sale as 'good quality dog food'. By mid afternoon he was throwing the money from the sale of the last bag of dog food into the till and smiling, *He always said he wanted to be a service to the community; well at least he has kept one part of the community happy.* At the end of the day the massive bone collecting lorry pulled into the back entry and Donald helped the driver push the metal container out into the yard. He watched as it lifted the heavy bones high into the air and tip them unceremoniously in amongst the tons of other animal bones. Soon they would be crushed into fertilizer and spread back onto the surrounding fields. *Yes, another fine service to the community you will make.*

The days turned into weeks and the weeks turned into months and no one made any enquiries into Jack's disappearance. He was listed as a missing person and as far as a police investigation was concerned, it had nothing to do with them. He had no reason to leave home and they had no reason to suspect foul play; soon the months turned into years and his disappearance remained a mystery.

Chapter 8

In the years that passed since his father's death and helped by the ever present Mrs Fairchild, Donald developed into quite an able businessman. He even had the foresight to employ a qualified butcher so that he could continue to fully learn his profession. And though it must have been on the minds of one or two of his customers, incredibly no one ever asked if he had heard any news about his father. It was as if the village was in collective denial.

Gradually, over time, the fact that Jack Wiseman had ever existed at all was just a faded memory, however, there was something not quite right. There was a growing anxiety about Donald that seemed to manifest itself in bouts of depression. So far he had managed to conceal things from everyone but the attacks seemed to be getting more intense and lasted for longer periods of time. By the time Donald reached the age of 25 he had rationalized that his condition was somehow connected to his subconscious and that his depression was brought on by the fact that he was missing out on some of the things that other people took for granted. So he hatched a plan to remedy his condition.

When the shop was shut, he would travel to neighbouring villages and try to find out what people his own age were doing. It wasn't long before the thought dawned on him that he was perhaps more attracted to members of his own sex than those of the female gender. That, in part, answered several of the questions about his state of mind which had thus far eluded him. Donald Wiseman was homosexual of that he was now certain.

One could perhaps be forgiven for thinking that a young man like Donald would find the realization of his sexuality liberating, but in his case nothing could be further from the truth; for without possessing the emotional and social skills to deal with it he was trapped in a world that he had no way of knowing how to get out of. *How did a homosexual go about finding a partner? How would he deal with rejection? What would happen if he made advances to the wrong person?* There were too many questions and far too few answers for him to deal with and in the end he dealt with it by letting himself go. Over the following days and weeks he rarely washed, cleaned his teeth or changed his clothes. He began to act like a tramp and people began to think that he was on the verge of some kind of mental breakdown, people began to stay clear of him and inevitably his business suffered. During the following weeks Donald descended into the worst depression of his life so far, but thankfully, his stone-cold will for survival kicked in yet again and he stayed alert long enough to know that he should sell his business before it became worthless. He put the shop and the house on the market and within the month he was back under the loving care of old Mrs Fairchild. She was getting on in years and for the last few years she had been virtually house-bound, but this all suited Donald very well. It would give him the cover he needed to re-build his life and emerge from his depression a new and very different man.

Chapter 9

Between the villages of Hamilton and Chiswick, there is a long and winding country lane. Both sides are festooned with plants and bushes of all kinds and colours. The lane itself is not wide enough for a car to travel along so, unless you cycle, the only way to get to the next village is to walk. In the winter, when the snow lies fresh on the ground and fields are crisp and white, it is a most beautiful picture, worthy of being on any picture postcard. At different intervals along the lane branches lead off to other places, farmers' fields, other villages and in some cases nothing but derelict buildings. In the height of summer most of the young local men and women gather to collect strawberries and again in October when the potatoes are ready to be harvested, thereby earning a little extra money. Quite often this gathering of folk led to friendships and sometimes even romance. This gathering would soon take on a prominent role in the life of one young farm worker.

About a mile along this lane, there is a fork leading off to the right. At this point you will see a pair of double gates, which are locked with a huge padlock. There is an eight foot high barbed wire fence all around the property to keep everyone out. Standing in the middle of this field is a derelict abattoir the same slaughterhouse where Donald's father Jack had worked after he served his time as a butcher. It had been donkey's years since it was last used, so naturally, the place appears to be considerably run down. The sign on the gate suggests that the buildings are unsafe and all-in-all people round about usually heed its stark warning.

There is quite a dense wooded area surrounding the abattoir and one's imagination could easily transpose the distant sight to that of a prisoner-of-war camp. The abattoir had been purposely built with its rear backing onto the trees making it virtually impossible for any straying animals to escape; consequently, there never were any rear doors to the building, thus making the front entrance the only way in and the only way out.

Two thirds of the way heading west along the perimeter fence, a combination of time, the elements and any number of vandals, have gouged a huge hole in it and it is through this hole that children would climb when they wanted to play in the trees. Occasionally they would shelter in the doorway of the abattoir but they never ventured further in. It looked too spooky in there and besides; the warnings of their parents' was enough to put off even the most daring child.

When Michael Brewer was about ten years old, he, and several of his friends would camp out on the fields on balmy summer nights. Their favourite pastime was sitting around a campfire eating sausages and beans and telling funny stories. How they would laugh at each other as each storyteller was faced with the expectation that their story had to be funnier than the previous tale. They were caught in that magical world that only children inhabit, a world of priceless wonder that is bought for nothing more than the cost of a can of beans and a few slices of bread. Many adventurous nights were passed this way when school was out, and continued right up to when the boys left school at 16. These were the images that Michael could see as he stood outside the gates looking into the field, hands in his pockets and a smile on his face.

Recalling all the happy times he spent as a boy, Michael continued his walk along the lane. This was his regular walk to the next village which he did every Saturday. Although a few years had passed since Michael and his friends had left school, they still met in Chiswick village square to re-live old times and seek out new adventures. It brought back a lot of happy memories.

As he walked along the lane, he noticed that the hole in the fence was still there, only it appeared to be a little larger, so it was not easy to miss or indeed to conceal as they used to do on camping nights so long ago. Michael looked around him, but there was no-one in sight. He wondered who had made the hole bigger and why. In the end he concluded that further generations of campfire story-tellers were the obvious culprits and with a shrug of his young shoulders, he ventured through the hole in the fence and into the field one more time with the voices of his friends from long ago once more alive in his ears. The only difference between now and in the past was the great care he took not to snag his trousers on the sharp edges.

Although he searched the immediate area thoroughly through force of habit, he could not find the piece of the fence that was missing as he always managed to do in the old days. He walked through the overgrowth and into a clearing. He stood in the middle of the field and scratched his head looking totally bewildered. It was as he lifted his head he noticed the abattoir doors were partially open. *Very strange* he thought. He was positive those doors were shut the last time he passed this way. *Who would be stupid enough to open those doors?*

He walked toward the building, cautiously taking a look around, but nothing seemed to be amiss. As he neared the doors, he felt a slight unease and once or twice thought of turning back. It was the thought of other youngsters camping in the grounds that made him carry on, he owed it to them to at least try to make it safe until the authorities could come along and seal the place up securely. It would have been better if he had listened to his inner voice and left things alone. Cautiously, he opened the doors a little further and took a hesitant step inside before stopping in the eerie silence. Waiting until his eyes became accustomed to the dark, he then ventured slowly into the room. His breath was heavy in his chest as his heart rate increased, his hands were cold and clammy by his sides and his ears strained for the slightest sound, he moved further into the building. About 50 feet in front and to the right, he came to the huge doors of the double refrigerator. It all seemed very strange to see something so big; it was almost surreal like Alice in wonderland. On the refrigerator doors was the biggest padlock he had ever seen. He took hold of the padlock and lifted it up, suddenly he had the dreadful feeling that he was being watched from somewhere in the shadows. He twisted the padlock this way and that and pulled on it to see if it would come loose, but it wouldn't budge and the doors were firmly locked. He let go of the padlock and it made an unearthly clanging noise as it fell back against the refrigerator doors, the echo of metal on metal clashed through the empty building and disturbed the roosting pigeons high in the rafters overhead. Their wings fluttered eerily in the darkness above him. *This is definitely odd, there is something wrong here* he thought as he took a few steps backwards towards the way he had come in, he did not take his eyes away from that refrigerator in all the time he was moving. When he felt there was sufficient distance between him and the refrigerator he shrugged his shoulders and half turned to make a dash for the entrance doors. As he did so, his blood ran cold as he heard a rasping voice carry through the darkness: "Stay just where you are if you don't want to die and don't turn around." Michael was rooted to the spot, he wanted to run but his legs refused to obey, he was trapped in the darkness and his mind wouldn't allow him to think. He should have carried on running but it was too late, his only chance was to reason with the formless voice…that was a big mistake.

"I saw the door was open and I just wanted to make sure the place was safe for the little ones." Those were the last words Michael ever uttered, a moment later a hammer smashed down through the darkness and cracked his skull wide open. In that terrifying instant, Michael Brewer was dead.

Chapter 10

Sunday morning dawned bright and sunny. The birds were singing in the trees and the flowers were blooming, but it had been a night from hell for the Brewer family. Never before had Michael stayed out all night without letting his family know where he was or who he was with, so of course, they began to fear the worst. Unknown to them, their fears were to be well founded because Michael's fate was sealed the moment Donald Wiseman watched him stumble through the hole in the perimeter fence.

Michael's mother and sister were crying and his father kept walking to the gate looking both ways along the street to see if he was anywhere in sight. By lunchtime, there was still no sign of him and they were getting desperate. At last Michael's father said to his wife: "That's it. I've waited long enough. I'm calling the police."

"Please John, not yet. He may come home by teatime," his mother cried.

"Mary, listen to yourself woman! None of his friends have seen him this weekend; they said he didn't show up yesterday. None of us have seen him. How much longer must we wait before you realise that something has happened to him? I'm his father, he is my only son. I feel it in my bones that something is wrong here. I'm calling the police." As the words left his mouth he was already halfway across to the telephone on the table in the hallway. He picked up the receiver and dialled. A voice on the other end of the phone spoke and, with tears of rage and frustration running down his face, John Brewer said simply: "I want to report my son missing; something terrible has happened to him, I just know it has."

He gave his address, his son's name and his description then, very slowly, he put the phone back in its cradle. Saying the words like that made him realise that his son was indeed missing and it was looking very serious. It was a realization that every parent must dread, the thought that your child may never be coming home again. Very slowly he turned, looked at his wife and daughter, sat in his armchair. He had no words left to say, he simply slumped into the empty chair opposite and quietly broke his heart. He knew for sure that his only son, his pride and joy, was dead. Mary and Madeleine ran to him, sat on the floor at his knees and cried with him.

Ten minutes passed in this way and just as they began to pull themselves together, there was a knock on the door. Madeleine went to answer it and found a policeman standing on the doorstep. She led the constable into the lounge to her parents. When John saw the policeman, he stood up and shook hands with Constable James Murray, a man who stood just a little less than six feet tall. Mary went into the kitchen to make a pot of tea, she had to keep busy otherwise she would go mad with worry. Constable Murray took the details from John. What Michael was wearing, his age, the colour of his hair, what colour were his eyes. Were there any distinguishing features, such as a mole, did he have a tattoo? Had they called other family members and Michael's friends? Had he ever done anything like this before? Every question cut into John like a knife because every passing moment wasted on questions was a moment that could be spent trying to find his son. Nevertheless, John steeled himself for the sake of his wife and daughter; he had to be strong for them even though inside he was torn to pieces.

Mary emerged from the kitchen with a pot of tea for them all whilst Madeleine sat in an armchair and let the tears run down her face. Eventually she said to Constable Murray: "If it will help, I have a photograph of Michael."

Constable Murray gently took the photograph and said: "Thank you Madeleine. This will help us a lot and don't you worry about your brother young lady, I'm sure Michael is safe and well. We will find him, trust me."

John Brewer was not so optimistic but for the sake of Madeline, he didn't speak his mind. *I feel it in my heart that he's dead. I only hope and pray that I'm wrong.*

That same morning, some children had found the hole in the fence surrounding the abattoir. They—like other kids before them—decided to explore it. So they climbed through the hole, then through the undergrowth and into the field beyond. Once in the open field they began running through the grass. They found that if they crouched down low enough they could actually hide in the grass as it had not been cut since the abattoir had closed down. They headed toward the trees, intending to climb them. One of the boys decided it would be a terrific idea if they checked out the old abattoir first. In his eyes it was an enchanted castle just waiting to be explored and inside there was all manner of wizardry and sorcery going on. It didn't take much to convince all the other children that it was the right thing to do, so they headed toward the building. It was a decision they would always remember…for all the wrong reasons.

As they pulled open the heavy old doors, they gave off that groaning sound of rusting metal and the kids laughed as they all pulled and pulled until the doors eventually opened enough for them to get inside. In all six children entered the abattoir with great big wary smiles on their faces, they chattered constantly about the many adventures they could invent in a place like that. They were chattering so loudly that not one of them noticed that little Hannah James had suddenly stopped walking and they all collided into her. Only then did they see what Hannah was staring at. There on the ground in front of them was the headless and handless body of a young man. At first they all thought it was a tailor's dummy, until they edged a little closer and saw dried blood all around where the head should have been. They ran from the building screaming at the tops of their voices and did not stop running until they all reached home. When the children told their parents of their find, of course they all thought it was a cruel prank someone was playing on the children to keep them away from the old building. Later that night, Hannah was asleep in her bed when suddenly she awoke screaming. Mom and dad ran into her room where they found her shivering and quaking and clutching at her sheets while she stared straight ahead and screamed. It took them over half an hour to calm her enough for her to tell them what had frightened her. She told them again of the body in the abattoir and how, although it had no head or hands, it had somehow got up to chase her. Mom and dad looked at each other and decided they had better check it out when it was daylight.

Next morning Hannah's parents asked if she felt she could take them back to the field. Very reluctantly and slowly, Hannah nodded her head. Mom and dad walked with her along the lane until they reached the hole in the fence. Hannah steadfastly refused to go any further. Dad told her to stay with mom and he went on alone to investigate. Ten minutes later, he came back and his ashen face told his wife that the children had indeed found the mutilated body of a human being.

Chapter 11

Chief Inspector Draylock was a big man in every sense of the word, hard bitten and no-nonsense, a man with a reputation for 'getting the job done'. He was of a heavy muscular build and stood well over six feet tall in his stocking feet. He had grey hair around the temples and burning brown eyes that had turned many a trainee police officer to jelly. He walked with a limp in his right leg, the result of a motorcycle accident some years previously, which would cause him some pain especially in the cold winter months. He was 55 years of age and nearing retirement age. He had been made a widower since his wife of thirty years had died two years earlier of breast cancer. There had been no children in the marriage although he and his late wife had always tried to conceive. When it had become obvious that they would never have children they accepted the fact and the subject was forgotten. It was only lately since the death of his wife that his earlier regrets had re-surfaced and he often thought how different things might have been.

He had been an inspector in the Wessex police force at the time of his wife, Sarah's death and in order to help him cope with her unexpected death he had asked for a transfer away from all the places that would remind him of the life he had shared with the love of his life for so long. To his surprise, along with the transfer came a promotion to Chief Inspector. More years than he cared to remember had been spent in solving crime in one form or another. He had witnessed death by fire, road accidents, brutal, mindless murder and suicide but nothing was to prepare him for what lay ahead.

Sunday was Draylock's day of leisure, the only day of the week when he had a chance to relax and recharge his batteries for the following week and to him it was sacred time. Living on his own, he rarely bothered to cook breakfast surviving on a cup of black sugar free coffee and a cigarette while he read the Sunday papers from cover to cover. That done, he would take a long hot shower get dressed and go to church. Although not a religious man, he had sought solace in the comfort of the church after his wife's funeral and the up-lifting optimism of collective worship seemed to prepare him for another week of crime-stopping. As he left the church, he shook hands with the vicar and commented on how he had enjoyed the sermon, something he did every week and the vicar would smile and thank him, knowing fine well that Draylock had not listened to a word he had said.

This particular Sunday had started like any other but that was soon to change; as Draylock left the church gates he almost collided with his sergeant John Davis who was moving swiftly in the opposite direction. Davis had been on his way home for Sunday lunch after just finishing his shift when he thought it would be a nice gesture to invite Draylock to join him and his family. He knew roughly at what time Draylock would be leaving the church so he hurried over to try and intercept him. Draylock was surprised to see him and even more surprised when Davis asked him to join them.

"Thank you John, I don't mind if I do, providing you stop calling me sir. I'm not at work today," Draylock smiled.

Davis nodded as he took his boss's elbow to turn him to the direction of his house, "It's a deal," he replied as they walked the 100 yards to the Davis household.

Mrs Davis had cooked a fine traditional Sunday roast with all the trimmings and after such a splendid repast there was little else to do except sit outside in the sunshine, drink an ice-cold beer and discuss the up and coming football match between Hamilton and Chiswick which was due to take place the following Tuesday. They laughed as they recalled the previous encounter blow-by-blow.

Mrs Davis suddenly interrupted their two-way commentary as she shouted: "John darling, there's a call for you from the station." Leaving Draylock to his beer in the sunshine Davis went indoors to take the call. Minutes later, he came back out again. Draylock looked up from his beer and said: "Nothing serious I hope, not on a day like this anyway?"

"A missing person," said John, "Apparently a young man had gone missing overnight. I've sent a constable along to take the details. I'll check them out later when I get back to the station."

"Why should they bother you with something as trivial as a missing person?" Draylock asked, "That's for the beat bobbies."

Davis shrugged his shoulders: "I don't know what it is but something has been bugging me lately and I can't shake the feeling off, maybe I'm getting paranoid in my old age, but I asked the desk sergeant to give me a ring if anything out of the ordinary came in. He's just doing what I asked that's all."

Draylock tipped his glass to his friend, "Can't fault you there my friend, good police work is ninety nine percent intuition and one per cent beaten confession!"

The two men talked into the afternoon until it was time for Davis to go back to the station to complete his split shift; at that point Draylock decided that it was time he went home. It was surprising he had stayed so long as he was not a man to outstay his welcome. Of course, it could have been the fact that he enjoyed watching John's children running all over the garden. Draylock had found it very pleasant listening to the children laughing, he had always imagined that scenario with himself at the hub of the family. To him there was no better sound than that of children's laughter. He thanked Davis and his wife for a very pleasant afternoon and began the half mile walk back to his own house. He put the key in the lock, opened the door, stepped inside and closed the door behind him. As he walked into his lounge, it hit him how quiet it was and how alone he felt. Spending an afternoon with a family had suddenly made him realise that perhaps he was ready to start living again; after all he wasn't too old for another run at family life.

He walked over to the drinks cabinet and poured himself a large whisky; he would think it through over a glass of the old mother's ruin. He was just about to settle down with his thoughts when the telephone rang. It was Sergeant Davis.

"Hello John, what can I do for you?" Draylock asked affably.

"Constable Murray has just returned with the details of the missing man and you know how earlier you said that good police work is all intuition."

"Almost all intuition," Draylock corrected.

"Yes well, I think this is one of those situations that we should move on quickly without waiting for the trail to cool down. I wondered which way you want to play this one?" he said.

"Do you feel that strongly about this?" Draylock asked.

"Yes I do,"

"Right, send a car for me because I'm half pissed." Draylock said as he quickly threw what was left of his whisky against the back of his throat.

He walked into the police station, much to the surprise of everyone on duty. He strode purposefully past the desk sergeant without his usual brief verbal exchange and straight up to his office where he found Sergeant Davis waiting. Whenever he was seen in anything like that quiet frame of mind his colleagues guessed that he was in 'focus' mode and very little else got through to him that wasn't within the radar of that intense focus. Davis looked up from the notes in front of him when he saw the massive frame of Draylock overshadow the light coming through the half glass door. As Draylock entered Davis stood up. "Right John," Draylock said, "What have we got so far?"

Together they went through all the information the constable had brought back. The circumstances of the disappearance seemed straight forward enough, but nothing is ever as plain as it seems. "Have you got the beat lads started on this yet?" Draylock asked.

Davis nodded, "I have had to keep things pretty low-key until we can officially move this up to a missing person stage, but I have told everyone working the beats to keep their eyes open and let me know if they see anything."

Draylock gave a slight cough, "Yes, officially that's all we can do right now, but unofficially I'm telling you to get your coat on so that we can get out there and have a look around for ourselves. Where was the lad last seen?"

And it was on that unofficial, low-key note that the biggest murder hunt in the history of the police force began.

Monday morning dawned cloudy and grey. The sky was overcast and a fine drizzle seemed to hang like mist in the air. David James, the father of the young girl who first found the body retraced his steps of the previous day to ensure he had not dreamed the events of yesterday. It was never clear why he didn't go straight to the police station screaming blue murder when he too saw the body, but people sometimes do the strangest things when they are in deep shock. He walked back out of the field, along the lane to Chiswick and straight into the police station. "Can I help you sir?" asked the duty sergeant who sensed immediately that this was no ordinary enquiry. "My daughter found a dead body in the old abattoir," Mr James said slowly and quietly. The sergeant looked at him and frowned, "Are you sure of that sir? Is it not just a dead animal or a dummy perhaps, put there by older children to frighten off the younger ones?"

"That's exactly what I thought at first," said Mr James as his voice began to tremble, "So I went and had a look for myself. This body has no head or hands and I need someone to take a look."

"All right sir. If you care to take a seat I'll get someone to come and take a statement." The sergeant was still uncertain of what to make of this apparent find so he asked one of the bobbies about to leave on his rounds to look after the desk whilst he went in the back offices to find a senior officer. He soon found one of his colleagues and he told him what Mr James had said. "Will you take a ride back out with him to check it out? It's probably a dead sheep or something," he said.

Draylock was just about to leave the office when he overheard the conversation that had just taken place. "It's all right sergeant. I'll speak to the chap, what is his name again?"

The sergeant shrugged his shoulders in surprise at Draylock's sudden interest: "Mr James, boss, he is out front."

"Show him through to my office sergeant and bring two coffees will you? Oh and hold all my calls."

"What shall I do if someone says it's urgent?"

"Do you really want me to answer that sergeant?"

"Er, no boss."

"Good, then show the gentleman in and hurry on with the coffee."

The sergeant had known Draylock for quite a while and he was used to his no-nonsense approach. He was a firm believer in tackling one job at a time and he wouldn't be rushed from up above or from down below. If he said "Do not disturb" he meant that even if the coming of the apocalypse was imminent he did not want to be disturbed. With that, the sergeant led Mr James through to Draylock's office and quietly closed the door.

It took Mr James several awkward moments to settle himself but Chief Inspector Draylock waited very patiently until he was ready to speak. "Can you describe what it is you think you might have seen Mr James?"

asked Draylock. Shaking very badly and wringing his hands. Mr James replied: "My daughter and some friends were playing in the field beside the old abattoir. She told me she'd seen a dead body but I didn't believe her, she is always making up silly stories and frightening herself half to death, but as time passed I became worried about her. She went to bed and had a real bad nightmare, so, the next day I asked her if she would show me where she thought the body was. When we got to the field she wouldn't go any further, so I left her with my wife and I went to look by myself. Beside the doors of that massive old refrigerator is a dead body, it's just a torso, it's got no head or hands." He put his hands over his face and said, "Oh God, I feel sick."

Draylock got him a drink of water and waited until he felt ready to continue. He watched as Mr James struggled to keep his shaking hands still, finally he managed to gulp down a mouthful of water and compose himself. Draylock took out his notebook and began taking notes. He asked what clothing, if any, the body was wearing and, as David James gave the description of the body, Draylock frowned. For some reason, this description seemed vaguely familiar to him. When Draylock had heard enough he thanked him and told him that he would find someone to take him home. "I would appreciate it if you didn't speak of this to anyone, especially the papers Mr James." Draylock said.

Mr James nodded and almost as if he needed evidence that it might be unwise to speak to anyone he suddenly felt the weight of Draylock's hand on his shoulder as Draylock slowly patted him for reassurance, "You have done very well Mr James, Oh and if we need anything further, also, would you mind if we speak to your daughter?" He added.

Mr James nodded slowly, "Yes, I mean No, not at all," he replied.

Draylock went up to the C.I.D. office and showed Davis and the other officers Mr James's statement. "Give me that description of Mr Brewer's clothing," he said. When he saw that the details matched he knew that the unofficial missing person enquiry had just become a murder hunt. At that point, no-one realised just how big this murder investigation was going to be, but they would soon find out.

Chapter 12

Later that same day, Chief Inspector Draylock and Inspector Davis walked along the lane that would bring them to the abattoir. Draylock wondered what he was going to find there although he had a rough idea. *If it has been there for any length of time it will have been gnawed at by rats and infested with all kinds of stinking parasites. How could a world that could be so beautiful also be so vile and ugly?*

They came to the hole in the fence and, after standing looking through it for a few minutes he climbed cautiously through into the field. Before going into the abattoir, he took a quick look around the outside but there appeared to be nothing amiss. The dirty drizzle that had earlier been heavy in the air had turned to rain and Draylock was almost eager to get into the building for shelter. Arriving at the front of the building, he cautiously pulled open one of the great rusting doors. Taking out his torch, he shone it inside through the gloom of the empty building. He had been told that the body was just beside the refrigerator doors, so that was where his torch first beamed to. *Strange, nothing there,* he thought. There was no body and, stranger still, on closer inspection it appeared that there was no evidence that a body had ever been there. *Could it really be kids playing tricks with a dummy? Could what Mr James thought he saw be just a figment of his hyped-up imagination?* Draylock had been a police officer for a long time and he had seen some strange goings on, but this was no childish hoax of that his instinct told him he was positive. *So what then? Where is the body?* He was just about to turn away when his eye was caught by something shining brightly in the torch beam beside the refrigerator doors. Bending down to take a closer look he saw that it was a man's ring. Because it was still bright and clean, it was obvious it had not been there very long. He took a small plastic bag from his pocket and slid his pen into the ring to pick it up. He began to look a lot closer at the ground outside the refrigerator doors and he saw what looked like a blood stain. "What do you make of this?" he asked Davis.

"It's a disused abattoir, it could be blood from anything," Davis said as he looked at the stain.

Draylock shook his head, "No, this is fresh blood and I would stake my life that it came from whoever this ring belongs to. It's either the killer or the dead man."

Davis didn't wait to be told what to do next, he took his radio from his pocket and called the police station for back-up and told them to send the forensics team along.

Whilst they waited for the back-up they went back outside and took a look around the immediate area. Draylock had a brief look into the trees but the falling rain deterred him from venturing any further.

"Shall I take a look in the woods Sir?" Davis offered.

"Don't be bloody silly Davis, rummaging around on my hands and knees in weather like this is not my idea of detective work. We'll leave that kind of shit for the snowmen. Let's get back in the doorway and keep dry until they arrive and set-up a decent mobile office, it looks like its going to be a long day. You had better ring your lovely wife and tell her not to wait up."

"What about informing the Brewers'?" Davis asked.

"And what exactly do we tell them?"

"We could tell them that, er…" Davis started to say before he was cut off in mid sentence.

"Yes, we could say to the Brewers' that we have been told that someone saw a body that fitted your son's description but it's gone missing again. How the hell would that make everybody feel, including me?"

Davis thought about how ridiculous it was to suggest that they should say anything at all. "What I meant, Sir, was that we should tell them that we have escalated our enquiries about her son's disappearance and now he is officially missing."

"Draylock shook his head and said: "That would only give them false hope, our priority is to find this body and then say what needs to be said to the family."

The two detectives stood impassively in the doorway of the old abattoir until the back-up team arrived and were quickly followed by the forensic team. Draylock directed them to the area near the giant refrigerator and asked them to start there and work outwards into the main floor area.

As he left them to their work he began to think of what Davis had said about informing the family and although he knew it was right to wait, he also knew that soon he would have to tell them the dreadful truth and no amount of police experience ever made that part of the job any easier to do. Despite his hard, indifferent exterior it was the one part of the job that he hated most. It's never easy to tell someone that a member of their family has died no matter what the circumstances are, but to

64

have to tell them that their loved one has been brutally murdered is the worst possible task of any police officer.

As the back-up team began to assemble the mobile police unit offices Draylock stood in the shelter of the doorway and watched the proceedings. With his hands in his pockets and his collar turned against the cold wind he tried to rehearse just how he was going to break the news to the family. It was no use; he decided that he would just have to use whatever words came when the time was right. He did however decide that it might be useful to go and talk to the family to see if they might be able to throw any light on things. In view of what he already suspected had happened Draylock needed to know if their son had any known enemies. With those thoughts whirling through his mind he decided that he would use the time waiting for the back–up team to set up to walk to the Brewer's home and talk to them.

As he was about to step out into the rain he spotted a young uniformed constable.

"Young man, go and get me an umbrella."

The constable looked bemused: "Beg pardon sir?"

"An umbrella man, I want you to get me an umbrella."

"Where from sir?" the young policeman answered.

"Use your improvisational skills," Draylock said.

"But sir, I wouldn't know where to start looking."

"How long have you been on the force young man?" Draylock asked dryly.

"Just over two years Sir," the young constable answered.

"Well, if you intend to be here for another two years you had better have an umbrella in my hand within the next five minutes."

With that the young constable dashed off in the direction of the hole in the fence. Within three minutes he reappeared armed with an umbrella which he triumphantly handed to Draylock. "One umbrella sir," he smiled.

Draylock looked at it and frowned, "It's a ladies," he said.

"A fine piece of detective work sir if you don't mind me saying so," the constable said with a cheeky grin.

"This is definitely a woman's umbrella," Draylock pointed out.

"You asked for an umbrella sir, you didn't say what sex it had to be. Besides if it's to keep you dry then a ladies one will keep you just as dry as a gents."

"What's your name constable?"

"It's Harrison sir."

"Well if you don't make it to Police Commissioner before you retire then I will eat my hat. And to whom do I return this umbrella when I have done with it? Draylock asked.

"WPC Makin sir; will that be all sir," Harrison smiled.

"For now," Draylock said as he opened the umbrella and stepped out into the rain.

He made his way to the hole in the fence and walked down the lane to look for Davis. He found him and told him to hold the fort until he returned but he didn't say where he was going. Davis busied himself organising the placing of the various caravans and mobile offices that had begun to arrive on the scene at the end of the lane. Draylock then set off walking along the lane in the opposite direction and in the direction of the Brewer's home.

He had been so deep in thought he had not seen Madeleine watching him walk up the garden path. She opened the front door so suddenly, that Draylock was visibly shocked out of his reverie.

"Hello, I am a police officer, are your parents home young lady?" he announced as cheerfully as he could. Very slowly, she nodded her head as she stood to one side to allow the policeman to enter. She walked into the lounge and said: "There's a policeman here Daddy with an umbrella like Mummy's." Draylock walked into the lounge behind Madeleine and introduced himself to her parents. He apologised for the umbrella as he explained that it was the only one available. John and Mary stood to shake hands with this big man standing in their lounge. They had gotten used to the idea that their precious only son was in some kind of trouble, but they would never have suspected the worst.

"Do you mind if I ask you some questions about your son?" Draylock asked.

Mr Brewer asked Madeleine to play up in her room whilst they spoke to the officer. Reluctantly she turned and left the room. He asked if they would describe what Michael was wearing on the day he went missing. They described his blue jeans and white trainers with a blue flash along the sides. His short sleeved white shirt. Michael's mother mentioned the ring always wore on the third finger of his right hand.

Draylock's hand moved towards the ring in his pocket but he did not take it out.

"Tell me more about the ring," Draylock said.

Mary didn't answer at first; instead she asked if Draylock would like a cup of tea.

"That would be lovely Mrs Brewer," he smiled. Then as she left the room he asked Michael's father about the ring again.

"It has his name inscribed inside it," he said. Then Mr Brewer said something that took Draylock by surprise. "Did you say that you were a chief inspector?"

Draylock nodded.

"Isn't that rather a high rank to be looking for a missing person?"

By this time Michael's mother had returned with a tray of tea. Draylock used the timely intervention to come up with a feasible answer.

"Well things are quiet at the moment and I was at kind of a loose end, so I thought I would take the chance to do a bit of old fashioned police work rather than push paper all day," he smiled, hoping that he had managed to sound convincing.

"We are just simple folk officer and it's not my place to say anything different, but I have the feeling that you are not telling us everything."

Draylock wanted to take the ring from his pocket again but once again he knew that without a body he was on very thin ice. After all their son might be holed up somewhere with the village hooker and here was he letting them think that he could have been murdered. Yes he had evidence that their son was in deep trouble and perhaps even dead, but without a body it was all circumstantial.

Michael's mother took a more direct approach than Draylock had expected.

"Is my son dead officer?" she said as her voice trembled.

"At this moment Mrs Brewer I don't know anything, we are doing everything we can to find out exactly where he is," Draylock said.

Mrs Brewer could hold in her tears no longer and the stress of the past few days flooded out into great sobs. Hearing her mother in such anguish like that made Madeleine dash down the stairs and into her mother's arms; somehow she knew that her brother would never be coming home again. John asked Draylock what he planned to do to find his son.

Draylock tried to change the course of the conversation away from the fact that their son could in fact be already dead. He asked what kind of man Michael was, about the things he liked to do. John said how he spent a lot of time with Madeleine patiently listening as she told him the things she and her friends had done. How he would help her with her homework.

"My son is a good boy Inspector," Michael's mother said, "please find him and bring him home."

Her words were hard for Draylock to take because he knew that he would be back there before too long with the news that he was already certain of. He drank the dregs from his teacup and rose to his feet and shook hands with the Brewers. As they led him to the front door, he told them: "I will find your son, that's a promise." With that he put up his borrowed ladies umbrella and stepped out once again into the relentless downpour.

Chapter 13

By the time Chief Inspector Draylock left the Brewer home the daylight was fading which added to the misery of the horrible day's weather. Putting his coat collar up, he walked back along the lane deep in thought about the events unfolding ahead of him. As he entered the lane he noticed someone acting strangely in the field to his right. In the distance he could see the lights from the police crews as they continued to set up their field offices. The shadowy figure in the half-light in the field seemed to be watching the police work being carried out. He stood and watched for a few moments hoping to get a good look at the stranger's face but it was too dark. Eventually he shouted at the man to stay exactly where he was. On hearing Draylock's commanding voice the man in the field turned around, saw Draylock looking at him and ran off in the opposite direction. Draylock could see that there was no way he could escape cleanly because of the trees, but he himself could not chase him because of the fence. *How the hell did he get in there, there must be a way in near here somewhere.* Draylock ran along the lane with his eyes still on the man, he cursed his luck as the man seemed to disappear against the trees. Suddenly he saw a tiny hole in the fence that was just big enough for a man to squeeze through. Once in the field Draylock headed towards the trees but he found nothing, he shone his torch around into the trees but too much time had elapsed since he scared the man off and he was probably back in Hamilton by then anyway. Draylock made a mental note to return in the morning to see if the man had left any clues to his identity but he knew that it was probably just some nosey local wondering what all the lights were up ahead. He made his way back onto the lane and dropped in to the abattoir to check on progress before he headed home. He found two uniformed officers at the entrance to the abattoir and they lifted a makeshift barrier to let him pass. Inside the grounds of the abattoir he made his way to a police caravan. There he found Davis talking to two officers from the forensic team.

"How did you manage to get this thing up the lane?" he asked, "I'm very impressed."

"I asked for a digger to make the lane wider so that we could bring things closer," Davis smiled, "No point in wasting good shoe leather."

"I suppose you put things right with the local conservationists first?" Draylock asked.

"Not exactly boss, but we can't allow a couple of displaced hedgehogs to stand in the way of police work can we?"

"If you put it to a referendum as to whether people would rather have policemen or hedgehogs I wouldn't bank on you keeping your job very long. So if anyone asks why we have ripped up a hedgerow I shall point them in your direction." Draylock smiled, "Now, where's the kettle, Sherlock?"

Davis poured Draylock a coffee and gave him an update before the two of them called it a day. As he was about to leave he put his hand into his pocket and took out the plastic bag with the ring in it. He handed it to the two forensics people and told them where he had found it. He asked for a report on it for first thing in the morning.

The following morning, Draylock and Davis went back to the abattoir, but before they left they had a meeting at the station with the rest of the team. Draylock had informed everyone, of the circumstances of the previous day. He also mentioned about the man he had seen in the field around the abattoir and he told everyone to be vigilant. He told them that everything depended on the forensic results as to what their next move was going to be. Someone suggested house to house enquiries but Draylock said that it was too early yet because he wanted to keep things quiet for the time being. If the murderer was a local man he didn't want him to panic and make a run for it. Draylock made it clear that he wanted this one solved quickly and with as little fuss as possible. With that he closed the morning meeting and headed for the abattoir.

As they neared the hole in the fence Draylock could see that it had been cordoned off as he had requested and there was a policeman standing guard.

"Everything alright?" Draylock asked as the policeman stood to attention.

"All quiet Sir," the policeman said as they passed on and headed for the front entrance. At the front entrance to the abattoir grounds Draylock was met by two other police constables, one of whom was Harrison.

"Anything to report Harrison?" Draylock asked.

"We've had reports of a string of strange sightings, Sir; apparently a man with a ladies umbrella has been seen acting suspiciously hereabouts."

"Very funny Harrison, I wouldn't mention that to the press if I were you."

"No Sir," Harrison smiled as Draylock and Davis walked towards the police caravan. On the way over to the caravan Draylock noticed that the doors of the abattoir were wide open, surely they should have been shut overnight? He walked back over to Harrison at the front gate.

"Has anyone been in the building this morning?"

Harrison shook his head: "It was locked up last night sir just after you left."

Draylock turned to Davis: "Did the forensic team search the building thoroughly yesterday?"

Davis looked a little sheepish, "I told them to concentrate on the blood stain; I saw no reason to search an empty building until we had more people here."

"That's bloody great news! For all we know we could have had the body and the killer right here under our noses all the bloody time. Get everybody over here now and get them in that building!"

"Everybody Sir?"

"Yes, everybody, I want that building searched from top to bottom and I want every damned inch covered twice!"

Davis had never seen Draylock so angry. He ran to the caravan and picked up the phone to the station. "The boss wants every available body over at the abattoir now, and he's angry as hell, so don't cross him."

Draylock entered the caravan just as Davis was putting the receiver down.

"They are on their way over boss," he said.

"I need a coffee, black and strong," Draylock said, "And when that crew arrive I want to speak to them before they go anywhere near that building."

Davis poured the coffee as Draylock sat fuming near the caravan window staring fixedly at the old abattoir. *That bastard I saw last night was the killer I just know it, he's making a bloody fool of me,* he thought.

Before long twenty or so extra police officers arrived at the scene and Draylock had them assemble outside the police caravan. He stood facing them and spoke from his elevated position on the caravan step.

"Now listen to me and listen very carefully. Just because we live in a part of the world where the only crime is kids drinking under age now and then doesn't mean that we have to act like bloody amateurs when something like this descends on us. We don't all knock off at five o' clock and sod off home in a situation like this. This is potentially a murder investigation and we not only can't find the killer, we can't even find the body! Do you know how that would make us look if the press got hold of this? Now, all this nonsense stops right here right now. I want every one of you to get your heads on this and start doing some serious police work and you can start by getting into that building and finding some results. And if I see one of you back out here without a bloody good excuse I will personally see to it that you serve the rest of your time in this force policing the remotest lighthouse island in the far north of Scotland; any questions?"

The stunned officers stood in silence, each man knew that Draylock was deadly serious. Without saying another word Draylock turned back into the caravan as the officers headed straight for the building.

About an hour passed before there was a knock on the caravan door, a young policewoman said they had found something unusual. Draylock and Davis followed her into the building. She led them to the far end of the building at the opposite end to where the giant refrigerators were. A light had been hastily set up and it was directed to what looked like a trap-door in the concrete floor. Two policemen lifted it and sure enough it was the entrance to an underground room. Draylock took out his torch and slowly made his way down the small flight of steps, there, tucked away in a corner, was a makeshift bed and a camping stove, there was also ample evidence that someone had recently been living there. Davis joined Draylock at the foot of the stairs and it was he who spotted what looked like the wooden shaft of a hammer sticking out from under the makeshift bed. Using a pencil, he carefully slid the hammer out from under the bed. Shining his torch onto it, he could clearly see tiny fragments of skin and what appeared to be dried blood on the heavy metal head. He called up the stairs for one of the forensic team to go down and collect it. There was no doubt in his mind that they had found the murder weapon, the only thing still missing was the body.

Later that day, it was confirmed that the blood and tissue on the hammer was from the same source as that of the blood stain found near the refrigerator. The forensic team also came back with news about the ring. Inscribed on the inside of the ring was the name 'Michael'. Draylock was absolutely certain that Michael Brewer was the dead man. *But where is the body that was here when Mr James saw it? Could the killer have returned to move it without anyone seeing anything?* Draylock stood in the silence of the caravan with his thoughts.

Finally turning to Davis he said, "Get the team together I need to speak with them again, we must find that body and soon."

Not far from the old abattoir there is a local beauty spot known as Shakleton's Clough named after the farmer whose land it bordered. It was an area roughly the size of two football fields and because of its combination of open space and secluded woodland it was a favourite spot with both young football stars of the future and of course clandestine young lovers. Because the area around the abattoir had been cordoned off to the public the local kids had migrated naturally to Shakleton's Clough and it was there one morning that the Sawyer brothers set up a game of football. The game had not been under way very long when a miss-hit shot went high into the air and came to rest well within the outer boundaries of the wood. It was Jimmy Sawyer who kicked it so it was up to him to go and fetch it. He put his head down and ran to get it. Although the wood has open paths criss-crossing through it here and there it is quite dense in other less frequently used parts and the ball had fallen into the dense undergrowth. Jimmy Sawyer wasn't the tallest boy by any means so his vision was as restricted as his height would allow, in other words he was hopeless as a lost ball scout. After a few minutes he had no option but to call on his team-mates for help. The other boys soon joined in the hunt, another couple of minutes passed before Jimmy laughed as he triumphantly held the ball aloft as he called to his brother: "I've got it Stephen, I've found it." Jimmy's older brother took one look at the ball and told Jimmy to drop it. Instead of doing as his brother said, Jimmy prepared to kick the ball back towards the pitch. He held it in his hands and only then did he see that he was not holding a ball... but a badly decomposed severed head.

76

He dropped the head and ran screaming to his brother. He was breathing hysterically by the time Stephen had managed to grab hold of him. He put his arms around him and held him close until he was calm enough to speak but it took a long time. Eventually Jimmy managed to speak through his intermittent struggle for breath: "Steve, what are we going to do?"

Stephen looked around at all the shocked, expectant faces, Stephen was the oldest and the other kids looked to him for guidance on all matters. He did not disappoint them.

"We don't say anything to anyone about this, do you all understand me?" he said in his most adult voice.

The row of faces nodded in unison. "Are we going to tell the cops?" one of the lads asked. Stephen told them to wait where they were whilst he went back for a closer look at the head. "Let's go home Stephen." Jimmy cried, "I'm scared."

"I have to make sure I know where it is if I have to tell anyone where it is," Stephen said as one of the other boys stepped up to take Stephen's place beside his little brother.

"Can you tell who it is?" one of them shouted.

"No, it's gone all black and it stinks," Stephen reported back.

"Can you see any bullet holes?" another called.

"Somebody find me a big stick," Stephen shouted.

"Are you going to whack it?" one of them shouted.

"No I'm not going to whack it. I'm going to stick it in the ground beside it so that I can find it again."

One of the boys picked up a stick about a metre long and threw it in the general direction of Stephen.

"God, I think its nose has been chewed off." Stephen said in disgust as he leaned on the stick to drive it into the ground as close as he dared to the severed head.

"What do we do now? Jimmy asked.

"I suppose we should tell dad and see what he says," Stephen said as he walked back to join the lads.

"What about my ball?" one of the lads called indignantly, "we can't leave it here my mum will kill me."

"Well if you want to go back in there and look around for it, be my guest, I'm going home to tell my dad." With that Stephen gathered up his little brother and headed off in the direction of the village. The boy whose ball it was hesitated for a moment or two before he took off with the rest of the lads, "Wait for me guys," he called nervously.

The boys made it home in double quick time and the group waited outside the Sawyer home as Stephen and Jimmy disappeared inside. Moments later a white-faced Mr Sawyer appeared at the front door and told them all to come inside. He told his wife to keep the children indoors all together until he had gone with Stephen back to the Clough to take a look for himself. The last thing he wanted was a horde of angry parents tramping all over what could be a murder scene. The stick was where Stephen had left it   and Mr Sawyer saw the horrible truth for himself. He didn't need any closer inspection to see that it was indeed a human head because the stench coming from it was gut-wrenching.

Father and son raced back to the house and called the police, within minutes three police cars sped into the street and the first two police officers to emerge from the leading car were Draylock and Davis. Mr Sawyer led the police to the gruesome find and the area was immediately sealed off. Draylock had every reason to believe that the head was that of Michael Brewer and he asked for a link up of the blood samples and skin samples found at the abattoir to be on his desk as soon as possible. He had a missing person, he now had a victim or part of one, so now that it was a fully operational murder enquiry he would have access to infinitely more resources and that would in turn lead hopefully to a swift arrest. Within a few hours Draylock would receive the first of many rude awakenings. And the first one was probably the most shocking and surprising of all.

After an initial examination and link-up tests, Chief Inspector Draylock was informed by forensics that there was no match between the head and the samples found on the hammer.

"Are you telling me that the head and the skin on the hammer might not be from the same person?" Draylock asked incredulously.

The forensic officer shook her head: "No, I am saying that they are definitely not from the same person."

"So this means we could have a double murder here?" Draylock said almost as if he were thinking out loud.

"That is exactly what it looks like," the forensics officer said, "So what now?"

"Well for a start it looks like we won't be able to keep this quiet for much longer." Draylock said as he nodded in the direction of the local news reporter who had just appeared on the far side of his office window.

"Shall I get rid of him?" Davis asked.

"No, show him in, we'll see if we can't reason with him," Draylock said.

Davis hung his head out of the office as the forensics officer went back to the murder scene and he asked the reporter to come into Draylock's office.

The reporter didn't wait to be asked to speak; he opened up his own enquiry with his own set of awkward questions. "Your people are crawling all over town, the abattoir is cordoned off and Shackleton's Clough is teeming with policemen in white boiler suits, what is going on?"

"Alright, now you listen to me, a body has been discovered and it looks suspicious but we would like you to play ball with us until we can make some delicate enquires," Draylock said.

"Surely you are not asking me not to report this, this is national news for Heaven's sake? Do you know how often a story like this lands in the lap of a mister nobody reporter like me? This is gold dust, this is my future," the reporter argued.

"This murder can be solved in a matter of hours, of that I am sure, but it means not spooking the murderer into taking off. If you print this we will have cameras from all over the world getting under our feet and every cheese-brained crank on the planet will be claiming to be the killer. Do you know how damaging all that will be?" Draylock asked.

"You can't keep something as big as this secret," the reporter protested.

"What is your name son?" Draylock asked.

"It's Matheson," he said.

"Well Matheson, I'll tell you what I'll do. If you keep a lid on this for another eight hours just to give us a head start, (he looked over at Davis when he realised his badly worded response) then I will give you an exclusive with all the details."

"And what if I don't?" Matheson asked.

"That would make you my first suspect young man and I would detain you for seventy two hours," Draylock smiled.

"Are you threatening me?" Matheson asked.

"You boys don't miss a bloody trick do you? Now do we have a deal or would you like cold porridge for the remainder of the week?" Draylock said menacingly.

"I'll give you eight hours from now and then it's a front page spread with your picture under the headline," Matheson said.

"Show Mr Matheson out Davis and show him where the cells are on the way by," Draylock said.

He was still mulling over the news about the head and the skin not matching up when another bombshell dropped out of the already darkening sky. As if that wasn't enough, he was still no closer to solving the crime when he had just committed himself and his team to finding the killer within the next eight hours before the world's media circus landed on his doorstep. *Perhaps its time to bring in Scotland Yard; but what do I bring them in to do that I can't do myself?* A myriad of thoughts and possibilities ran through his mind as he tried to summon all of his police experience to help him out, but it was no use, all he could do was return to the abattoir to see if anything else had turned up. Perhaps his presence on the scene would be good for the morale of the team; after all they had been working round the clock for the past few days.

As he arrived at the abattoir nothing could have prepared him for the news that he walked into. The police officers searching the area around Shackleton's Clough had found more grisly remains, but they were not the remains he had expected, in total another four human heads had been found among the trees. Draylock knew now beyond any doubt that he was dealing with a multiple murderer and he wondered how many more there were. The other burning question was where the rest of the mutilated bodies were? It was time for another team meeting.

Draylock gathered as many of his team together as he could without stopping the on-going search. "First of all I want to thank you for your hard work and dedication so far, it has not been easy for any of us. No doubt you all know by now that we have a maniac on the loose and might I add it is one who so far has proved to be very clever, he is confident enough to move freely around without any apparent fear of being apprehended. And besides being totally deranged he is highly dangerous, even more so by the fact that we have not got any idea of his identity. So besides extra vigilance and care I want a complete search of the whole area. Not one inch is to be missed and I want anything you find, no matter how small. I don't care if you think it may have nothing to do with this case, I want everything brought back to the office for examination. Be responsible for yourself and for your colleagues, look out for one another and don't approach anyone alone.

The last thing I want is anything happening to one of you lot. Right, let's get started."

Draylock left the men to it and drove back the police station to wait on the forensic reports on the other victims. Unknown to the officers working in the abattoir and in the surrounding fields, Donald Wiseman was sitting in the rafters high up in the roof, he had made himself a hideaway above a false ceiling and from there he could see their every move and hear their every word, he sat there like some God in Heaven…watching the poor mortal fools below him.

Unbeknown to Draylock and the police searching the fields Donald Wiseman had been moving freely amongst them almost from the very start of the investigation. It didn't take a genius to work out that the majority of the policemen were wearing either white or blue overalls and white face masks most of the time. All he had to do was steal one and he had a ticket to visit all areas of the crime scene. No one stopped him and no-one questioned him. All he had to do to move to and from his hideaway high in the rafters was to wait until the coast was clear.

As he watched the teams disperse after the team-talk Donald decided it was safe to climb down and see for himself what progress was being made. . He had just reached the top of the ladder when he heard some of the police returning. He quickly flattened himself to the heavy steel girder beneath him and he held his breath to listen. It was a false alarm, the voices passed the door and he was free to make his way down again. He climbed down to the floor and made his way carefully toward the open doors, all the while looking back to be certain that no one had seen him. He looked into the distance and headed towards the far side of the abattoir grounds where most of the activity seemed to be going on. He pulled his mask over his face and joined the working group. He had not been working for long when he and the rest of the team heard a commotion over by the abattoir building. A young constable was standing at the abattoir door shouting that he had found something. It didn't take much for the other officers to stop what they were doing and go to see what it was all about.

The constable was pointing to the rafters, "Up there, I have found a room where someone has been staying; there are knives and hammers and biscuit wrappers and empty crisp packets."

Damn! Donald thought; *they have found it; someone is going to pay for this.*

As the other officers filed in to take a closer look and congratulate the policeman who found the hiding place, Donald slipped away unnoticed…but he had no intention of staying away for long, he had business to conclude.

Most of the police work over in the trees had been done, the area had been picked clean and gone over until not one blade of grass had been left undisturbed, to Donald that gave him the perfect place to hide. He ducked underneath the police tape telling people to keep out and he hid among the trees watching the policemen leaving the abattoir obviously hyped-up by their find. He watched as the forensic team brought out evidence that they thought would convict the killer when they brought him to trial. *They will have to catch me first.* He waited in the trees until darkness fell and until the activity in the abattoir faded to just the odd policeman moving from the abattoir over to the caravan or to the mess room that had since been set up. If he was going to make a move, now would be his best chance. He waited a further few minutes until he was absolutely sure that only one or two police officers had been left behind to watch over the scene. He ducked back under the police tape and began to make his way warily over to the main building.

When Draylock heard about the find it gave him a massive boost, but it also gave him an embarrassing headache. When he was presented with the items collected from the rafters from the abattoir, he was relieved yet angry, "How the hell were these missed, and how the hell was this second hiding place not discovered until now, three days into the investigation? My explicit orders were to search every inch of that place," he shouted at everyone in the office back at the station. "What makes things worse is that the killer has probably been watching us, I dread to even contemplate the thought but perhaps he has even been moving amongst us!" He took a few deep breaths as he searched the faces of the officers until he calmed himself down, he could tell from the expressionless features looking back at him that he had well and truly made his point, "Anyway, I have to say well done. At least now we know what weapons he used and I'm sure we can find fingerprints on some of this lot," he said as he swept his arm over the evidence on the table in front of him.

Meanwhile Donald was still moving towards what was now an almost deserted main building. It was a moonless night and the only light he had to be wary of was the light coming from the windows of the police caravan in the distance. He reached the main building and flattened himself against the wall as he saw, not twenty feet in front of him, a solitary policeman guarding the main door. Silently and unseen Donald moved along the wall until he was just a few feet from the unsuspecting constable. The constable seemed to be doing a kind of sentry routine, he was stepping a few feet outside of the door before turning back to stand in the open doorway of the abattoir. Donald watched him do this from the shadows two or three times before he decided that it was time to strike. The constable heard a footstep behind him, but it was just a little too late. As he was about to turn around, he felt an arm go around his neck, a sickening twist and a crack followed as his neck broke instantly. In an instant the unfortunate constable lay dead on the ground. Donald noticed a coffee cup with the fresh warm coffee giving off a wisp of steam just inside the doorway. That explained the constable's furtive movements as he walked in and out of the doorway. An evil grin formed on Donald's lips. *You were having a sneaky drink weren't you? You naughty policeman, that's why you were walking in and out, to see if you were being watched. Well you were and now you are dead!* He picked up the dead man's coffee and drank it while looking at the body in front of him. The body had fallen right across the open doorway so when Donald finished his coffee he took hold of the feet and dragged the body outside. He placed the constable's left hand behind his neck and he put the coffee cup in his right hand and balanced it on his chest, then he crossed his legs at the ankles as if the constable was having a lazy afternoon nap.

"There now, all your friends will know just what a lazy little pig you are, fancy sleeping on the job." Donald said as he calmly sauntered off into the darkness.

Chapter 14

Constable Danny Bulmer was due to relive the dead constable just before midnight. As usual he used his bicycle to get to and from his work. He made his way to the abattoir and as he reached the main door he suddenly stopped and let his bicycle fall to the ground. He walked slowly towards the dark figure on the ground just outside the main doors. His heart skipped a beat and a look of shock and horror came over his face when he recognised his friend and colleague constable Turner lying there in such an odd manner, it was obvious that there was something seriously wrong. He knelt down beside him and felt for a pulse in his neck, the moment he touched his friend he knew that he was dead. Instinctively he stepped away from the body and quickly took his radio from his belt, and radioed to headquarters. Within minutes, the area was once again covered with policemen.

Draylock was as angry as hell that morning as he strode up and down the incident room. "What the hell was he doing there by himself?" he shouted, "Did I not give specific orders for no one to be out there alone? How do you lot think I am going to tell this young officer's parents that their only son is dead, killed because of the incompetence of his colleagues? Because you failed to carry out my orders, a young promising life has been cut short, another statistic added to the list of this maniac who is still running free and apparently able to kill anyone he likes at will, and right here one of our own right under our bloody noses. The bastard even had time to position the body to give himself a sick laugh. I want the bastard caught, and quickly do you hear?" As he spoke the last words, he strode to the door and almost tore it from its hinges. "Now get out there and do what you are supposed to do." The shocked congregation of officers quickly filed from the room, never before had anyone heard him raise his voice, let alone lose his temper.

The rain was falling down heavily on the day Constable Turner was buried. His coffin was carried into church on the shoulders of six officers as a guard of honour stood at each side of the pathway, each policeman saluting a fellow officer and each one had a tear running down his cheek. After a packed service paid glowing tributes and said farewell to a fine young officer his body was laid to rest. Several people stood outside the church gates looking in as the funeral cortege entered…among them was Donald Wiseman.

When the funeral was over, Draylock—with his head bowed and his hands in his pockets—walked away from the church, vowing to catch the man responsible for the murder of a brave young officer. *This should never have happened, not on my watch.* It was a vow he intended to keep…even if it killed him.

Within minutes of hearing of the murder, Draylock had organised road blocks and alerted the airports and ferry terminals. Although he knew that his killer was probably still close by, he couldn't take any chances. He had no idea who he was looking for, so he could offer no description for the authorities to watch for, all he could do was ask them to report any suspicious looking characters.

Despite a massive police investigation a full month went by without them being any closer to catching the killer than on the first day of the investigation. Draylock was becoming more and more frustrated. With the death of the police officer the story had broken, Matheson had done his job with gusto and the media wasted no time at all in dramatising every minute detail. The village resembled a formula one gathering with all the media caravans and heavy-duty camera trucks rather than a sleepy picture postcard setting and the whole circus was adding to the frustration and hindering the investigation. On top of all that, sightseers and ghoulish souvenir collectors were roaming all over the place and the inevitable false confessors crawled out of the woodwork and had to be painstakingly questioned before being eliminated. All of which took time and effort and resources which were already stretched to breaking point. He needed a breakthrough or he would have to involve Scotland Yard. Draylock was not to know that very soon he would have the breakthrough he needed.

Chapter 15

When the Sawyer brothers found that first head they knew that it was obviously serious, but they could have had no idea at all of the full awaiting consequences. Once the huge police search was fully underway nine other skulls had been unearthed. The skulls were in varying degrees of decay suggesting that the killings had been going on over a very long period of time. It was strange that in such a small, close-knit community no one—until the Brewers—had reported anyone missing. There was another strange aspect of the case which was creating a major mystery, where were the other body parts? Despite all the police efforts with the latest technology and specially trained sniffer dogs they had managed to find nothing. Finally—after it was decided that the area was clear, the police decided to abandon the search for further evidence and the area round the abattoir and Shakleton's Clough were returned to the general public.

The news soon hit the newspapers that the search was soon to be "dramatically scaled down" as they put it. Most people—including Donald Wiseman—knew that was official 'police talk' for calling the investigation off because they were no closer to catching the killer than on the first day of the investigation. As the search winding down, Donald couldn't resist taunting the police one more time and it was very nearly his undoing.

He made his way to the lane to watch the police taking away their mobile units and field mess rooms. There were other people about so he felt safe, a lone figure may have attracted attention, but with others there he could easily blend in.

He stood close to a small group of people who had gathered to watch the police moving out. It was as one officer was walking towards the main entrance that Donald had the surprise of his life. The young officer stopped and asked Donald what time he was going to be back on duty. Donald looked at him with a blank expression on his face.

"What do you mean?" he asked.

"I mean what shift are you on?" the officer asked.

When Donald looked at him in silence with a confused expression on his face the officer carried on, "You are still working out here aren't you?" he asked.

For once Donald was flustered and all he could think of saying was: "I'm just going to visit my mother in Chiswick."

"Has the old man given you the day off you lucky dog?" the young policeman asked with a smile.

"I don't know what you mean," Donald said.

"You are with the force aren't you? I have seen you working out here, you must be with forensics." The young policeman asked. Donald felt an icy hand grab his heart; he knew that this officer must have somehow seen him in the grounds of the abattoir posing as a police officer involved in the hunt for clues. *Come on Donald think!* He began to tremble inwardly and he prayed that his body wouldn't give the policeman cause for suspicion. Donald looked at the young officer and motioned with his eyes that perhaps they should not be talking like that with so many civilians around. The officer suddenly remembered where he was and he fell for Donald's ruse. "Oh, hang on a minute; I think I have mistaken you for someone else," the young officer said as he back-pedalled, he was convinced that Donald was a police officer on some kind of undercover surveillance and he thought that he had almost given the game away.

"I had better be getting along," Donald said as the officer turned sharply to rejoin his colleagues who were about to leave the grounds of the abattoir for the last time. It had been a close call, too close for comfort Donald thought, but the episode had given him the rush of adrenalin that his body had been missing since the murder of Constable Turner.

Draylock arrived on the scene five minutes after Donald had left, perhaps if he had been around at the time things would have been very different. Draylock had turned up just to take one final look over the scene that had been his life for the past several months, and, come so very close to defeating him. He wanted to brand the image of that desolate place onto his mind to make him even more determined to solve those horrific crimes. Draylock stopped to speak to the young officer who minutes earlier had been chatting to Donald. "Everything alright Mundy?" Draylock asked.

"No change sir, everything is squared away and quiet," he answered, "I hope I haven't blown it sir," he added.

"Blown what son?" Draylock asked bemused.

"Our man's cover sir, I went over to chat to him without realising that he was on duty."

"What are you talking about Mundy? Draylock asked.

"One of our lads was standing with a group of people over there by the gate and I asked him what he was doing and when his shift started. I didn't stop to think that he was working undercover."

"What did he look like?" Draylock asked.

"About my age and build." Mundy answered.

"Would you recognise him again?"

"Of course I would sir, easily. Have I done something wrong sir?" Mundy asked.

"Quite the opposite, it could be something and nothing, but we don't have anyone working undercover. Make your way to the station tomorrow and I will get the team together to see if you can pick him out, if not then I will need a full description of the man you spoke to. It's too late in the day now, first thing in the morning will do." With that Draylock phoned Davis and told him to gather everyone who had worked at the abattoir in the past two months to meet in the sports hall on the following morning.

Donald meanwhile thought he was in the clear; he had outsmarted them yet again. Instead of going home he decided to hide out in the woods and circle back to the abattoir when everything was finally quiet. By nightfall everyone had gone and an eerie silence descended on the place. The shadow of the sinister old building stood out dark and imposing against the blue of the night sky. It was a clear, cloudless night and the moon was in its third quarter. Donald waited a while to make sure no-one would come back before he stealthily made his way back to the abattoir. He found the doors had been closed and locked with a heavy padlock but that didn't pose much of a problem to him. He shinned up onto the roof of what was once the security lodge at the side of the main doors and very gingerly slid one of the corrugated roof panels up far enough for him to drop down into the deserted abattoir. It was an escape route that he had made for himself years earlier, and one that he had never needed until then. He stood motionless in the gloom; there was no light or the slightest sound. Complete and utter silence surrounded him. Very slowly he ventured further into the abattoir, his ears straining for any movement at all. The strange hum of deathly silence was all he heard. Eventually he reached the trapdoor in the floor which had once housed his bed. He lit his torch and looked around at the empty room; the police had taken everything. *Bastards, they have even taken my bed!*

Undeterred by having nowhere to lay down he stretched out on the floor where his bed had once been. He was gazing up at the ceiling…when he first heard the noise. His heart seemed as though it had suddenly stopped as he jolted up-right to listen again to the sound. *What the hell was that?* He listened again but heard nothing further. *It must have been the wind in the rafters.* He lowered his body back onto the hard floor and no sooner had it made contact than he heard the noise again. His eyes widened in the darkness and moved immediately over to the closed trapdoor above him; he fully expected it to be flung open at any moment and a team of armed officers to bear down on him. He held his breath and waited, but again nothing happened. Then, there it was again, the same noise. *Where was it coming from? Who was making it?* He began to panic. The third time he heard the noise was too much for him. He jumped up and huddled in a corner. *If it was the police they would have been onto him by now, so who was it?*

Slowly, he began to recover his nerves; he decided to venture out into the main building. Slowly he made his way up the steps and lifted the trapdoor letting it fall open noisily onto the old concrete floor. The clashing noise reverberated all around the empty building as he climbed out and stood once again in the silence. Suddenly he heard a whispering sound behind him. "Who's there?" he demanded. The whispering voice broke into a sinister laugh. He tried to shake the sound from his ears but wherever he turned the voice followed. By then he was really scared. He began to shout: "Who are you? What do you want? Come and get me if you can or leave me the hell alone."

The disembodied voice did not answer; instead it swirled around his head until he could do no more than clasp his hands over his ears and fall to his knees. His eyes bulged as he tried to see his tormentor, but he was alone…or was he?

Chapter 16

The first person Donald had killed after his father was a young man. He had met the young man by chance while visiting the site of his old home. No-one lived there anymore and it had never been re-built so all that remained was virtually a burned out shell. The young man had been standing looking at the ruins of the house when Donald came by. Donald told him he used to live in the house and asked if he would like to see inside. Donald said that he could give the young man an idea of how it looked when it was at its best. The young man was curious to know how such a fine building could have been left like that and he told Donald that he would like to take a closer look. The two of them walked into the house through what remained of the front door archway and Donald showed the man the layout of all the downstairs rooms. Over in the far corner of the hallway were the badly charred remains of the staircase.

"Would you like to see what is left of the upstairs?" Donald asked as he pointed to the staircase.

"Is it safe?" the young man asked.

"Oh yes, it's quite safe, that old staircase was made from oak, it will still be standing long after everything else has turned to dust," Donald said. The young man's eagerness to see upstairs clouded his better judgement and before he knew it he was on the landing at the top of the stairs. Donald pointed ahead to what was formally the master bedroom. "That was my mother's room," Donald said.

"Which was your room?" the young man asked.

Donald pointed to his right, "This was my room," he said.

The young man entered and stood just inside the door, it was then that Donald made a pass at him. He reached out his hand and touched the young man's hand. The young man thought at first that it had been an innocent touch but as he pulled his hand away and looked at Donald he realised that he clearly had other intentions.

"I have to leave now," the young man said bluntly. To which Donald became angry. He had never had a girlfriend and it was on the spur of the moment that he decided that he would try his luck with a young man. The shock of having his sexual advances rejected unnerved him and he was suddenly sickened by his own actions.

"I'm sorry," he whispered as he hung his head and stood to one side to allow the young man to leave. The young man made for the open door but as he was level with Donald he picked up a heavy brick that had fallen from a crack in the wall and he smashed it into the young man's head. The ferocity of the single blow killed him outright. To Donald's surprise he found that the killing had given him a sexual satisfaction that he had never before achieved in his life.

After the killing, the problem of identification and where to put the body were what concerned Donald. He reasoned that to cut off the head would prevent identification, so that would not be a problem, but there were also the hands. Fingerprints were also a way of identification, so the hands would be cut off as well. It was then that he realised that he had the perfect workshop right there on the outskirts of his own village.

It wasn't that difficult to get the body back to the abattoir where it was hung upside down by one of the hooks in the rafters. With the body in place ready for dissection, Donald proceeded to cut off the hands first. This part of the process was easy for him because of his butchers training. Once the head was cut off, he decided to bury that among the trees at the back of the abattoir and the torso was put inside the huge refrigerator until he could decide the best way to dispose of them. He also found a very ingenious way of disposing of the hands, what he did with them exactly Draylock would find out in due course.

The villages of Hamilton and Chiswick were well known for their casual work during the summer and autumn harvest months, so there was a constant supply of victims for Donald to choose from in the years that followed, that was why no one reported people as missing. However, the disappearance of Michael Brewer was to change all that and that fundamental mistake was about to haunt Donald Wiseman in more ways than he could ever have imagined.

Donald was still standing at the entrance to the cellar in the abattoir trying to identify the voice that had returned with a vengeance. The spirit of Michael Brewer was watching from the rafters as Donald dragged himself to his feet and walked in circles around the blacked out abattoir. By now he was like the frightened child he had once been cowering at the very thought of his drunken father returning from the late night drinking sessions. "Is it you, you BASTARD?" Donald called at the unseen voice. As he called out the voice took on a hissing sound and other noises echoed around the building. The sound of footsteps was joined by high-pitched laughter, the sound of doors opening and slamming shut, was accompanied by images of his former belongings being strewn about. He couldn't tell if the things he was seeing and hearing were real or if they were the maniacal ranting of his own warped imagination. The cacophony continued until Donald collapsed into a snivelling, frightened heap on the floor. He lay there until the din finally faded away, with the last whisper of laughter he took his hands from his head and looked towards the roof where he had dropped through earlier, he had to leave that place, or he would go completely mad. As he got unsteadily to his feet he heard a deep guttural chanting sound coming from within the cellar and that signalled the start of another spiritual assault. This time the voices were manifold swirling and thrashing around his head as he tried in vain to beat them away. The ghosts about him had him trapped and they knew it. They took their turns at swooping down on him and screaming into his tear-stained face. Donald summoned all of his strength to climb up the wall to reach the loose roof panel that he had entered the building through, he pushed at it frantically until it gave way and opened, he rolled out onto the low roof and almost threw himself into the grounds of the abattoir, his nightmare in the haunted abattoir was over…or so he thought.

Chapter 17

Although the abattoir had not been used for over ten years until Donald rediscovered it, there was still the smell of death in the air and that to him seemed like an added attraction. Still in place were the foundation walls of the holding pens where the animals would be kept for a day after transportation. In these pens the animals would be calmed overnight so that when they were slaughtered on the following day their meat would not be deep red as it would have been if they were slaughtered whilst still in a state of anxiety. There were also signs of the cutting rooms where the animals were dissected, visible too were the troughs in the floors for the blood to drain away, the hooks in the overhead beams where the carcasses hung were still exactly as they had been left. All in all it was the perfect place for Donald to live and to hide the bodies of his victims until he was ready to dispose of them.

The abattoir had originally been built away from the villages because no-one wanted to be down-wind of the stench of hundreds of animals waiting to be killed and no-one wanted to hear the sound of cattle, pigs and sheep squeal as their throats were cut while hanging upside down. That wasn't exactly how the animals were slaughtered, but in the imaginations of the general public that is precisely how the deed was done. Every cry that comes from an abattoir is the sound of an animal at the point of death. And to hear lambs being gathered for the chop is not the most pleasant sound one would wish to hear, they can sound uncannily like new-born babies in distress. Despite the abattoir owners doing everything they could over the years to please the public eventually, due to pressure from the expansion of the surrounding villages, the abattoir was closed down completely and had been allowed over time to fall into disrepair.

Donald was very pleased when he came across the disused abattoir. It suited his purposes perfectly. Most deserted places house either mice or rats. This one had rats, lots of them and very big ones at that, but for some reason they never ventured near the part of the abattoir that Donald called home. Rats are well known to be sensitive creatures and they pick up on forces that humans are unaware of. That's where the saying about rats leaving a sinking ship comes from. Occasionally, a rat would venture into the area, sniff the air and, squealing loudly, run back to its own part of the building. Donald had witnessed that strange phenomenon on more than one occasion; *I wonder what it is about this section that scares them,* he thought.

That night Donald made his way through the grounds of the abattoir towards the home of Mrs Fairchild, he had lived there ever since she had been kind enough to take Donald in again after he had to sell his business. Night had fallen and Donald was lying on his bed trying to clear his mind and hopefully find sleep. He had barely closed his eyes however when a voice very close to his ears whispered: "I'll make you regret killing me. You should not have done that. I had a life to live and you took that away. Now you will pay." Donald was petrified, he jumped out of his bed and ran outside onto the landing; he tried to be quiet so as not to wake Mrs Fairchild. The voice followed him onto the landing so Donald ran quickly down the stairs. He tugged frantically at the front door until it finally creaked open. A blast of icy rain blew into his face and took his breath away but he felt as though he had no choice but to escape. He would rather be outside in the rain than in the house with that sound.

In his demented state, half scared out of his wits, he reasoned that if the voices had followed him home then his second home back at the abattoir must be clear. He ran out into the driving rain and headed back to the abattoir. He climbed back onto the low roof and once again dropped down onto the floor below. All night long, he huddled against the cellar walls drenched to the bone until, as dawn finally broke, he decided to go back out to the main building. Hugging his arms around himself, he took a tentative step outside, ears straining to hear the slightest noise. He was wet, hungry and so very cold. Not a sound could be heard anywhere, not even the sound of a solitary bird outside in the breaking dawn. He looked back to the open trapdoor and decided that he wanted to sleep. The relief he felt as he fell onto the floor where his bed had once been was phenomenal. He imagined himself pulling the blankets right up to his chin; he rolled himself into a ball and instantly fell into a deep sleep. This was not a peaceful sleep however. He had been asleep for only two hours when the dreams began. Bad dreams, in which he could see the faces of each of the men he had killed, and they were all laughing at him. Tormenting him with cries for mercy, one moment he was cursing them with all the venom he could muster and in the next breath he was pleading with them to leave him alone. He wanted to run away and hide forever, but where to? *Through the fields and into the trees behind the abattoir, no, not the trees, there are heads in there, there are faces in there*. He dare not stop

102

to look around him. Behind him, following him, heads and hands, clutching at him, reaching out trying to catch him. No bodies, just him screaming at the top of his voice. He awakened, covered in sweat and screaming. Somewhere in the abattoir, the distant sound of laughter rings out.

Chapter 18

Three days had passed since the police moved out of the abattoir, but to Draylock and his weary officers it seemed like it was three months. Draylock stood at the window of his office, it was raining hard and he watched the rain fall onto the dull street below. He had his hands deep in his pockets and a thoughtful look on his face. *All those dead people, how in heavens name are we going to identify them all when we don't know the first thing about them?* he thought. And what was worse there was still no clue as to who was responsible for this carnage. The fingerprints found at the scene were not those of a known criminal and not for the first time Draylock was beginning to question the way the investigation was going. *Were his officers up to it?* They had the will and plenty of enthusiasm for the job, but enthusiasm is no substitute for hard gained experience.

He turned from the window and looked at Davis who was busy looking through a file, "There has got to be something that we are missing, there must be something that this maniac left behind, no one is that perfect."

"We have been through everything boss with a fine tooth comb, a fly couldn't fart in that place without us picking it up," Davis said and he carefully placed the file he was looking at on his desk.

"Have we organised the line-up in the sports hall yet, the one that I asked for three days ago?" Draylock asked sarcastically, knowing full well that there had been a problem.

"You said you wanted everyone there at the same time boss. Have you any idea how long this takes to organise with people on sick leave and holiday?" Davis protested.

"When will people round here start to realise, I mean, when will the bloody penny drop that this is a murder investigation not a bloody crèche?" Draylock fumed.

"The men are tired sir, they need a break." Davis reasoned.

"What about the relatives of the dead men? When do they get a break from wondering if its one of their children that we have found? I want everybody who has worked on this investigation in the last two months to be in the sports hall at eight in the morning and no feeble excuses. And tell Constable Mundy to have his wits about him because I want either a positive ID of the man he saw or I want an accurate description."

Draylock suddenly stopped his impromptu rant when he saw Davis looking back at him with a blank expression of despondency on his face. "Yes I know I have given you an administrative mountain to climb, but you must know that I wouldn't ask you to do it if it wasn't vital."

Davis nodded, "I know Boss; I will have everybody there at eight, leave it to me."

Draylock pointed his fingers at Davis in a mock cowboy pose and made a clicking sound with his tongue. "Right," he said, "go home and have a good night's sleep. We have a long day ahead of us."

Back at the abattoir, Donald was quickly beginning to realise that his reasoning that the voices were elsewhere was misplaced. He was tired and hungry and afraid, but something told him that he would be safe so long as he stayed put. He was too scared to sleep, but either his willpower was not strong enough or sheer exhaustion got the better of him, either way, he fell into a deep sleep. Sleep came easily but it was not peaceful for long. He dreamt he was walking through familiar fields; he turns on hearing voices calling his name. He can't tell for the life in him if it is the voice of his beloved mother or that of his hated father, the voice is echoing in the breeze all around his head. Then, headless and handless corpses rise up from the ground, from unmarked graves deep in the earth where they have decayed into grotesque skeletons; they somehow recognise him as their killer and they close in on him. He begins to run, he can't stop he has got to escape. No matter how fast he runs the bodies keep coming after him, he has nowhere to hide. Wherever he turns the bodies block his path. *There will be safety in the trees if I can just make it to the trees.* The tree line approaches and he turns to see that the pursuing tormentors have been left far behind, the trees have saved him. He stops to catch his breath and leans against a tree. Suddenly the tree turns into a headless body and wraps its vice-like branches around him holding him tight. He looks out in horror at the steadily approaching bodies as they sweep towards him over the open field. In amongst the trees behind him he can sense the heads watching and waiting for him to move again. Maniacal laughter begins to emanate from the mouths of the eyeless heads to accompany the thought that he is finally trapped with no escape. The slow, lingering laugh at first gradually builds into a loud thunderous roar straight from the bowels of Bedlam.

Donald came awake with a start and thought he could still hear the laughter in his head. It was so loud that, try as he might, he could not block out the noise. Very slowly, Donald forced his eyes to focus on the effervescent glow which was forming into a shape in front of him. Then, out of the shape, came the ghost of Michael Brewer. Donald began to cry, loud, pathetic racking sobs escaped his throat: "Who are you? Why are you haunting me? he cried pitifully. A voice reverberated around his tiny cell as the figure disappeared. "You know who I am and you know why. There are countless reasons why. I told you I would make you suffer for taking my life. You will never be free of me. By the way, I've brought some friends to see you." As he spoke, the headless bodies of each and every man he had killed began to appear, each one was more grotesque than the other. As the last one appeared covered in blood where Donald had so cruelly and callously hacked off its limbs, Donald ripped at his hair with his trembling hands and screamed at the top of his voice for them to leave him alone. The voice of each dead man swore a curse on his name as his mind descended into a whirlpool of murderous visions until his mind could take no more; finally he collapsed into an unconscious wreck on the hard stone floor.

Several minutes later he awoke to find he was alone again, his tormentors had vanished. Slowly and painfully, he arose from the floor with eyes and ears straining for any sight or sound. Thankfully there just the sound of the wind high in the rafters above him.

Chapter 19

Chief Inspector Draylock awoke the following morning to the sound of rain running down his window. He got out of bed and, as he stood at the window watching the rain, he thought of the day ahead and what he was going to do, hopefully the identity parade would turn up something. *I hope Mundy did his police training well,* he thought.

He had a look of sheer determination on his face that morning as he walked into the station. There was an air of anticipation and excitement about the place as scores of officers began to arrive, everyone wondered what was going to happen. Davis was perhaps the first to notice that rare look on Draylock's face, it usually indicated that something big was about to happen, because that look on his face made big things happen.

Mundy was brought through into Draylock's office the moment he arrived and Draylock ordered coffee. "I have over two hundred officers in the sports hall Mundy and they will soon be given instructions to file past you and speak to you. Now what was it that the chap you spoke to at the scene said," Draylock asked.

"The most recognisable thing he said was, 'I'm just going to visit my mother in Chiswick'," Mundy answered.

"That will do," Draylock said, before he turned to Davis and said: "Right, get that out to everyone in the sports hall, they are to file past Mundy on my signal and say that line in a loud clear voice. And let them know that if I hear one Mickey Mouse or Wallace and

108

Grommit impersonation I will personally kick their arses into the middle of next week."

"I've got that boss," Davis said as he went off to prime everyone in the sports hall.

"Are you ready for this Mundy?" Draylock asked as he drank the last of his coffee.

"I'm ready sir." Mundy said.

"Just remember, take your time and let me know the moment you see him," Draylock said as he held open his office door for Mundy. The two men walked along the corridor towards the sports hall like two condemned men. Draylock looked every inch the distinguished officer, but inside he was shaking like a rookie on his first riot patrol. He could feel it in his bones that something was going to turn up.

Davis had set up the identity parade well and judging by the co-operative silence which descended on the room when Draylock entered his comments had also been relayed verbatim.

Mundy stood facing the officers as they filed past him one at a time. Once eliminated the officers were free to either go home or resume their duties. While this was going on, Draylock sat in his chair watching and waiting. It was mid-morning when the last of the officers left the sports hall, the man that Mundy saw at the scene was not amongst them. Draylock's feelings were ambivalent, one part of him was disappointed with the outcome of their morning's work and another part of him was happy that he at last had a suspect, or at the very least a suspicious set of circumstances surrounding as yet an unidentified man. Draylock, Mundy and Davis cut lonely figures in the huge sports hall; it has been a strange experience for everyone concerned even the officers on parade, many of them didn't even know why they had been called to the hall anyway.

"So what do we do now?" Davis asked.

Draylock raised his thumb: "Now we find a police artist and make a mug-shot of our friend who went to see his mother in Chiswick."

"I don't mind if I never hear that phrase again sir," Mundy said with a weak smile.

"You did well young man, just keep your concentration until after the artist has taken some details and I will treat you both to a few drinks tonight, how does that sound?" Draylock smiled before he added, "God knows we could all do with a break."

With that they left the sports hall and headed back to Draylock's office. Just before midday an artist appeared and he and Mundy set to work, within half an hour—and although he didn't know it—Draylock was looking at an almost identical picture of Donald Wiseman. "Is this the man you saw Mundy?"

"Without a doubt sir, that's him," Mundy nodded

Draylock thanked the artist and handed the picture to Davis: "Send this to reprographics and have a copy sent to every station, post office and community centre within a fifty mile radius, I want to find the man in this picture."

"What about the press sir?" Davis suggested

"Yes, the press, TV the whole shebang, I want to find this man and talk to him and I have a feeling he is still near-by," Draylock said, "Now, get your coat on Mundy because I owe you a drink, today we will rest and tomorrow we will find our man…that's the plan any way.

Draylock took Mundy over to the local pub and they were soon joined by Davis.

"Is everything going alright at reprographics?" Draylock asked.

"Yes, that side of things is fine, but I'm not sure it's a good idea to have a drink just yet," Davis said.

"Why not?" Draylock barked, "We have bloody well earned it."

"I agree sir, but the press and TV will want a statement and it might give out the wrong impression if we are all half cut when they turn up."

Draylock laughed: "It would certainly give them something worthwhile to write about, that's for certain. But let me deal with them, all things have a time and a place and my time and place is right here right now, the real work and the press and TV statements will come soon enough tomorrow. Tonight is a night off for us so enjoy it." With that the three men began a drinking session that lasted until the early evening. Draylock was feeling merry after several pints of Chiswick's finest ale and he bade his colleagues a good night just before nine pm. The rain was steadily falling as he made his way to a waiting taxi that would take him home before midnight—and in a relatively good mood—for the first time in months.

Draylock made himself a strong coffee before he turned in for the night; he had promised himself a night off but he was wise enough to know that he had to keep one eye on the bank of pressmen and TV presenters that he would have to face before very long. He knew that the publication of the picture of a suspect would make headline news and Davis had made a good point; that he had to appear on top of his game.

He slipped into bed and turned off the light for what he hoped would be a restful sleep…but that night, he got far more than he could ever have expected.

He was in that twilight zone between sleep and consciousness that we often visit just before sleep takes over when he heard what he thought was a voice calling his name. He opened his eyes and strained them to peer into the darkness: there it was again, and there was no mistake, "Draylock." He sat up onto his elbow and turned his ear to the window. *If that is that bastard Matheson from the local press trying to get the edge on everyone else I will arrest him and throw away the bloody key.* His first thoughts were that Matheson has somehow got hold of the story early and decided to call on him at home to get a statement. It was then that he realised that Matheson had no idea where he lived. As these thoughts were going through his head the voice spoke again. "Draylock, my killer is in the abattoir, go NOW!"

Draylock knew that he had had a few drinks but no way was he that drunk to have voices in his head. "Who are you?" he asked.

"GO NOW!" the voice demanded. Draylock threw back the covers and picked up the phone. His fingers automatically went to Davis's number.

"Hello Davis is that you?" he shouted at the stunned voice of Davis on the other end of the phone.

"Yes it's me boss, what's the matter?" Davis asked.

"We have no time for questions, order a car from the station to pick me up now and get them to collect you on the way over. I want another three units with us and no sirens." Draylock demanded.

"Where are we going?"

"I'll tell you in the car." Draylock said as he put the receiver down and started to get dressed. It was unlike him to act like this but the voice he heard was too distinct. It had been right there in the room with him and he knew he had nothing to loose by reacting to it. Something told him that the voice was far more than his subconscious mind acting on his eagerness to catch his killer.

Within minutes Davis was parked in the street outside Draylock's house with three other units and six burly officers.

"I brought six good men," he said as Draylock ducked into the back seat.

"Where to boss?" the driver asked.

"To the abattoir, and park at the end of the lane, I don't want to announce our arrival, I've done that too bloody often lately," Draylock said.

Over at the abattoir Donald who had not dared to move for a full 24 hours was woken by the sound of driving rain hitting the old tin roof; he prayed that it wasn't a prelude to his tormentors' return. His eyes were suddenly drawn to the same effervescent glow that had visited him on the previous night, it was over by the far wall of the cellar but this time it was different. Instead of forming into the shape of a dismembered body it formed into the shape of a human head. It had ghostly features and as it looked at him with blood-shot eyes its mouth curled into a spine-chilling grin.

Donald screamed and ran out of the cellar and into the main building he climbed up the wall and tore frantically at the roof to squeeze out onto the low roof outside. He hung his body from the gutter by his arms and let himself drop and he fell right into the waiting arms of two of Draylock's officers. Draylock took the artists picture from his coat pocket and shone his torch into the unkempt face of Donald. A smile lit up his face as he turned the picture to Donald, "Do you recognise this chap?" he asked.

Donald said nothing. Draylock motioned with his head to the abattoir doors and said to Davis: "Let's get those open and see what delights there are inside shall we?"

Davis stepped forward, lifted the heavy padlock and turned the key; two officers took hold of the doors and pulled them open. By this time Donald was securely handcuffed to the two officers. "What is your name?" Draylock asked.

"Donald Wiseman," Donald said, "and that's all I'm saying," he added.

"Calm down Donald," Draylock said matter-of-factly, "that's all I asked." Draylock went into the abattoir and made sure that Donald was taken back inside too. Once inside Draylock's eyes were drawn to the faint glowing light still emanating from the cellar. Donald had visions of the head and began to panic. He tried to pull away from the officers but without success. Draylock looked at Donald, "Shall we take a little walk?" he said as he motioned in the direction of the cellar with his head. Donald began to visibly tremble, "I can't go near there," he sobbed.

"Oh yes you can," Draylock said dryly, "my officers will escort you."

"But there's a head in there, it's got no eyes and it's laughing at me. Please don't make me go there, please," he begged.

Draylock walked to the top of the stairs leading down into the cellar, then, turning to the officers holding Donald he said: "Keep him here."

Just as Draylock was about to climb down the stairs he heard the sound of laughter from way up above him in the rafters. He turned back to the officers, "Do you hear that?" he asked.

"Sounds like someone laughing sir, I've heard it before in here; I think it's the wind playing tricks with the roof," one of them answered.

Draylock looked back into the darkness below his feet and remembered the voice that he heard not one hour ago in his room, the voice that told him to go back to the abattoir and find the killer. He wasn't the kind of man to believe in ghosts but he was certain that there was some kind of strange and powerful force at work. It was then that the same voice he had heard in his room spoke again, but this time, only he could hear it.

"You now have the man who took my life."

"Did you hear that?" Draylock asked again. This time the officers shook their heads. Once again Draylock began to go down into the cellar. At the foot of the stairs he could see the faint glow of the strange effervescent light, as he stared into its midst it began to pulsate and grow stronger.

"Let me get out!" Donald screamed from up in the main building.

"Shut him up!" Draylock shouted, as he looked at the emerging face within the light. "Who are you?" he asked.

"I am Michael Brewer. And the man you have is my murderer," came the distant reply. Draylock watched as the light began to fade until darkness pervaded the cellar once again.

"Are you alright down there sir?" Davis called.

"Our work here is done chaps," Draylock said as he emerged from the cellar, "let's get this man back to the station: read him his rights Davis. He is under arrest for the suspected murder of Michael Brewer."

Davis read him his rights and he was taken back to the station. It was four in the morning when Draylock and his team finally got back to bed and their day would start again before seven in the morning. With Donald safely locked up Draylock thanked the small team of officers who had been involved in the arrest. He told them to be prepared for a hectic few days and he advised them not to talk to anyone about the arrest or the suspect. The last thing he did before he left was to tell the duty sergeant to have Mundy report to his office first thing in the morning, his evidence would be vital.

Chapter 20

Early the next morning Draylock was back in his office with Davis and Mundy.

"Have forensics come up with any matches?" was the first thing Draylock needed to know.

"Nothing yet," Davis said.

"Then a positive identification of the man you saw will be a good place to start Mundy, are you ready to take a look at him?"

"Yes sir," Mundy said.

The three of them went down to the cells. Donald had been moved earlier in the day into a cell with a two-way mirror. The first thing Mundy saw was the back of Donald, he had curled himself up on his low bed with his back to the mirror.

Draylock spoke to the duty officer and told him to wake Donald up. The officer went in and shook Donald. "On your feet and face the wall," the officer said coldly. Donald stood up and looked at the wall. "Is that him?" Draylock asked.

"That's him boss I'm one hundred percent certain."

"Do you need to hear him speak?" Draylock asked just to be sure.

"No sir, that's him."

Draylock was relieved, all he needed then was forensics to come up with evidence that he was the killer and he could wrap up the case within the next few hours. However, things were not going to be that simple. Donald had spent his whole life avoiding detection in some way or another and just as Draylock was a skilled and determined policeman, Donald was no slouch when it came to self preservation and cunning. He also knew that he had covered his tracks very well indeed, after all, only he knew where the bodies were.

Before Draylock started to question Donald he needed some evidence from forensics, yes he had a positive identification from Mundy but what did that prove?

Back in his office Draylock stood over by the window with his hands dug deep in his pockets. His head was bent forward and rested on his chest and he was deep in thought. Draylock knew that Donald was indeed the murderer but, without concrete evidence from forensics—which he didn't yet have—he could not even hold Donald let alone charge him. Davis knew only too well the predicament Draylock was in.

"We could go for the confession without evidence sir," Davis said.

"We might just have to." Draylock said as he turned from the window, "But something tells me that this guy is not going to be an easy nut to crack, I think he will push us right down to the wire."

"He came in limp enough last night Boss," Davis offered, "he was like a lamb to the slaughter."

"All we got out of him last night was his name and if you remember that was all he was going to give us," Draylock said cautiously. Just then there was a knock on the office door, it was the duty sergeant. "Sorry to bother you sir, but Wiseman is making a hell of a racket downstairs, he says he wants his lawyer."

"I knew it, I knew it, the bastard has started his capers already," Draylock said.

"Shall I tell him he can see his lawyer?" the sergeant asked.

Davis interrupted: "To hell with it Boss, let's call the bastard's bluff, let him call his lawyer, even if we don't have anything, they won't know that will they? And if we start playing for time he might get cocky and clam up completely."

Draylock thought for a moment, he could see the sense in Davis's tactics but what if Wiseman pulled the double bluff and they came up short? "Yes, we will go with it, sometimes things happen by chance and we are on a roll I can feel it. Yes Sergeant, get him his lawyer and let's draw a line in the sand. Let me know the moment he arrives."

With that the duty sergeant left and Draylock started to prepare his line of questioning. It was then that Davis asked about the strange goings on of the previous night. "Boss, what made you think of going back to the abattoir in the dead of night?"

Draylock was caught off-guard and he had no ready answer, he couldn't very well say that a ghostly voice had told him. Instead he made light of it: "Elementary my dear Davis I worked on the assumption that a murderer always returns to the scene of the crime. I figured that the press and media coverage would keep him quiet for a while, but that his urge to kill would still be as strong as ever, so my dear Davis, it was frustration that forced him back to the scene of his crimes, any criminal psychologist worth his salt will tell you that to relive your crimes in the place they were committed is very often a good substitute for the real thing. That could also be the reason why there are still so many missing body parts, who knows, perhaps we shall know soon enough when the lawyer arrives." Draylock's pastiche of Sherlock Holmes paid off and Davis was satisfied with his plausible explanation. Either way he gleaned that it was the only explanation he was going to get.

Just after lunch the duty sergeant looked up from his desk to see a very well dressed young woman standing in front of him. Her blonde hair was swept back from her lovely fresh face and collected into a bun at the back, she smiled at the sergeant and he was momentarily lost for words. He finally broke the awkward silence: "Can I help you madam?"

"I certainly hope so sergeant," she smiled, "My name is Elizabeth Ogylvie and I am here to see my client Mr Donald Wiseman."

She could have knocked him down with a feather. *How on earth could Wiseman get himself a stunner like this to represent him?* he thought. "But you're a woman," he said, without thinking how ridiculous he sounded.

"How very observant of you sergeant," she said with a polite smile which disguised her contempt for his ignorant assumption implied by his response.

"Could I see my client now sergeant?" she added. "My time is costly."

The sergeant squirmed with embarrassment as he quickly ordered a policewoman to escort her through to an interview room to wait for her client. In the same moment he picked up the phone to Draylock. "Wiseman's lawyer has just arrived and just to warn you sir, she is a woman."

"Did she give you her name?" Draylock asked.

"Elizabeth Ogylvie."

Draylock told him to let her know that he would be down to speak with her and her client after they had had an hour or so together.

Just my luck, he thought as he replaced the receiver, *I'm sure she is the daughter of Sir Kenneth Ogylvie one of the best legal brains in the country. I am going to have my hands full with this one.*

"Are you alright Boss?" Davis asked.

"I was until about two minutes ago, the brief he has employed is likely to chew us up and spit us out without any concrete evidence, we need something more, and fast."

Draylock took in a deep breath as the hour was almost up, and together with Davis he made his way to the interview room. Besides the smell of Wiseman, the first thing he noticed was how stunningly beautiful his lawyer was. He looked at the two sitting side by side and couldn't help but fleetingly reflect on the stark contrast between them. Here was she, graceful and elegantly refined and there was he, unwashed for days, perhaps even weeks and looking as though he had been haunted by all the demons from hell for the past ten years.

Draylock hardly had time to sit down when Ogylvie tried to open the proceedings and gain the advantage with a forceful attack.

"I believe my client has been arrested on suspicion of murder," she said.

Draylock was having none of it: "Good afternoon Miss Ogylvie, how are you today?" Draylock smiled.

"Actually it's Mrs Ogylvie," she replied icily.

"Oh I do apologise, I thought you were the daughter of an old adversary of mine Sir Kenneth Ogylvie."

121

"Sir Kenneth Ogylvie is my husband, so I would prefer it if you addressed me as Mrs Ogylvie, my correct title, from this point onwards."

"As you wish Mrs Ogylvie," Draylock said calmly. *Sir Kenneth Ogylvie, the lucky old bastard!* he thought.

"So Inspector, what evidence do you have?" she asked.

"Actually it's Chief Inspector Mrs Ogylvie, so I would prefer it if you would address me by *my* correct title from now on."

Yes, first blood to us! Davis thought as he listened intently to the opening gambits.

"So *Chief* Inspector, what evidence do you have linking my client to any murder?" Ogylvie asked.

"Let's take things one step at a time Mrs Ogylvie, I would like to ask your client a few questions about why he was trespassing last night." Draylock said in an effort to steer clear of the evidence issue. Luckily Ogylvie took the bait.

"Oh come on Chief Inspector, that abattoir has been a regular short cut for donkey's years and everyone knows that. If you are trying to press murder charges relating to his *alleged* trespass then you will have to arrest every dog-walker from Hamilton to Chiswick on the same charges." Ogylvie said.

"Not quite Mrs Ogylvie, there is a marked difference between taking a short cut and breaking and entering a securely locked building, your client arrested as he was climbing out of a building that he had obviously been living in for some time and we have clear evidence of that, it was me that he almost landed on top of when he jumped down from the roof. I would like to ask your client what business he had in that building."

At that point she turned to Donald and said: "You don't have to answer any questions at all if you are not happy with them."

Donald looked at Draylock and said: I got drunk and lost my way, I fell asleep in that building and I have no idea how I got there, the next thing I knew I was being handcuffed by two of your men, and they hurt my arms."

Ogylvie interrupted Donald there and spoke to Draylock: "Am I right in saying that my client offered no resistance to your officers?"

"He offered no resistance," Draylock conceded.

"And are you aware of the injuries to my client's wrists due to the excessive force used by your officers?" Ogylvie asked.

Donald lifted his arms to show the ugly blue bruises around his wrists.

"They are bruises Mrs Ogylvie, hardly life threatening and they were caused when your client was reluctant to come back into the building that he had just climbed out of, those so called injuries were caused by your client, not by my officers. But if he wants to see a doctor then I'm sure I can arrange for him to see the police surgeon later."

"I have a better proposal," Ogylvie smiled. "Why don't you charge my client with murder or trespass or both and then get him the medical attention that he is entitled to. Or don't charge him and let me take him to the hospital to have his alleged *self inflicted* injuries looked at?"

"He hasn't answered my question yet." Draylock said.

"He told you he was drunk didn't he? That is a reasonable answer. Now Chief Inspector, I must ask you to either charge my client or let him walk out of here with me this minute." Ogylvie smiled.

Draylock rubbed his chin with between his finger and thumb as if he was mulling over his next move. In reality all he was doing was buying an extra few minutes in the hope that forensics would deliver the goods. "Would you excuse us for two minutes Mrs Ogylvie?" he asked as he motioned to Davis to step outside the room. The two officers went into the corridor outside the interview room leaving Donald and Ogylvie alone.

In the corridor Draylock was getting visibly agitated.

"Don't you just want to punch the smug bastard?" Davis said.

"Yes but I would never hit a woman," Draylock said.

"I meant Wiseman." Davis laughed.

"I know you did Davis and I suppose this is no time for jokes, but she has us over a barrel and she knows it. Where the hell are forensics when you need them?"

"So what do we do?"

Draylock thought for a moment: "We let him go, and we put a man on him, I want him watched twenty four seven and if he so much as farts in the street I want him hauled in for pollution. Two can play at her game."

Ogylvie was as surprised as anyone when Davis returned to the interview room alone and told Wiseman that he was free to go. She had asked for him to be charged fully expecting the police to do just that, it was now obvious that her challenge had paid off and they had nothing to hold him on. Donald too was equally surprised at how easy it was to just walk out without so much as hint of a sweat-down. *Perhaps those things only happen in the movies,* he thought as he and Ogylvie were leaving the room.

Outside the station Donald asked her what he should do next.

"You can thank Mrs Fairchild for employing me for starters, she insisted on having only the best for you, she has known my father for many years and she says that you are like a son to her."

"She took me in when I was young." he said.

"My services come at a very high price, so she must think highly of you, I hope you don't give her cause to be let down. And one more thing, don't talk to the press no matter what they offer you, because they only print what they want to print no matter what you say and they do have the power to sway public opinion if they choose to do so."

"Thank you for everything Mrs Ogylvie." Donald said weakly.

"Actually it's Miss Ogylvie," she smiled.

"But I thought back there…"

"Yes I know what I said back there…I lied, just to poke the Chief Inspector off balance, it's a woman's prerogative."

Back inside the station Draylock was looking down at the couple from his office window.

"Davis I want our best surveillance team on this guy, I know he's our man and I know that he will make a mistake. When he does, I will be there to take him out."

Chapter 21

Donald was exhausted. He made his way home to his room at Mrs Fairchild's house. She greeted him on the doorstep like the biblical father of the prodigal son. She looked around as she ushered him in and once inside she offered him everything but the fatted calf.

"You look dreadful darling," she said as she ran her fingers through his matted hair. "You need a hot bath and a good meal."

"I just need to sleep for now," he said.

He went upstairs to his room and lay on the bed fully clothed. It had been a long day and an even longer night. He was so very glad of the chance to rest and catch up on some lost sleep. *No ghosts can get me in here*, he thought…

Draylock was still cursing his luck when the phone in his office rang; the monitor on the phone told him that it was forensics.

"I hope this is good news," Draylock half growled down the receiver before anyone had chance to speak.

On the other end of the line was a young woman who had worked on the case since day one, her name was Helen Tate and she was exceptionally good at her job. Draylock had a soft spot for her and they usually took every opportunity to flirt with each other outrageously.

"Hello Chief," she said, "I hope you are sitting down?"

His voice softened when he heard her voice, "I really need you to say something to cheer me up."

"Well I heard a rumour that you are really good in bed," she said.

Draylock laughed out loud, "Only you could get away with that with the mood I'm in, does this mean that I'm not going to be happy with the next thing you tell me."

"Boss, that guy must have been wearing a space suit when he killed those men, he hasn't left a trace of anything to go on, we can link the murder weapons to the tissues of some of the victims but we can't link the murder weapons back to him," she said.

"Have you tried everything?" he asked.

"We have sent samples off to Germany and America, but it will take a few days before those results come back," she said.

Draylock could sense the lack of optimism in her voice. "You don't sound too hopeful of them finding anything, am I right?" he asked.

"Am I that easy to read?" she said.

"So what can we really expect from either of them?" Draylock said ignoring her question.

"We send things to each other in particular instances just as a kind of back-up, you know, fresh eyes and that sort of thing, but in all honesty, they won't find anything that we have missed, he's as pristine as a new born baby," she said.

Draylock sighed and sat back in his chair, "In that case, tell me what you are wearing under your lab coat," he said.

"Why don't you pop over and see for yourself?"

Draylock laughed again, "Twenty years ago young lady and you would have been in big trouble, I would chase you to the end of the world."

127

Helen blew a kiss down the phone and said: "I'll let you know when the results come in from America and Germany but don't hold your breath."

Draylock put the phone down, she hadn't given him the news he wanted but she had certainly cheered him up and it bolstered his resolve to crack on with the immediate job in hand which was to watch Wiseman like he was under a microscope.

Davis had called on Sergeant Knox—one of his best surveillance men—to watch Wiseman and report on his every move. He was parked in the street outside Mrs Fairchild's house when Donald made his way up to his bedroom. He watched as the light went on and he waited for the light to go off again…but it didn't. Unknown to him Donald was too afraid to put out the light even though he felt safe in the only real home he had ever known. Since Mrs Fairchild had taken Donald and his father in all those years ago Donald had become the son she never had and although she knew that he had some emotional issues she put that down to him losing his mother and the trauma of the fire. In short, she doted on him and in her eyes he could do no wrong. She was horrified to learn that he had been arrested and she didn't hesitate to employ the best defence that money could buy. She also had connections in the area and she knew how to use them.

Knox had been on stake-outs before and he thought he had seen everything there was to see but nothing could have prepared him for the bizarre story that was about to unfold in the Fairchild home. Knox had been watching the bedroom window for about an hour when he thought he saw a shadow move across the line of light, at first he thought it must be Donald walking around so he noted it down that there was movement and he did nothing more. It was then that the light went out and the strangest thing happened. The room seemed to light up again almost immediately but it was a very different kind of light. Knox noted that the light in the room had been replaced by a glowing, pulsating light; he thought perhaps that it was some kind of sun-bed.

Inside the bedroom Donald was about to wake to the shock of his life. His bed began to shake as though an earth tremor was rocking the whole house. His eyes opened and darted insanely round the room. There standing over him was the spirit of Michael Brewer in all his menacing glory.

"Leave me alone!" Donald screamed. It was such a high pitched scream that it resonated right throughout the house. Mrs Fairchild hurried to the foot of the stairs and called up to Donald but there was no answer. The spectre of Michael glowed even stronger, almost as if it was feeding off Donald's fear.

Michael's voice boomed out through the room: "I will leave you alone when you tell the world what you have done to so many innocent young men."

"I will never tell!" Donald hissed.

Michael leaned in to the cowering Donald so that he could see deep into his eyes: "I want to know why you killed me; I want to know why you ruined the lives of my mother and father and why you ripped the heart out of my baby sister? You have condemned them to a life of sorrow and unless you confess I will bring all of hell into your every waking minute."

Mrs Fairchild could hear voices in Donald's room but she couldn't make out what was being said, slowly she began to climb the stairs. Donald somehow summoned the courage to face the ghost of Michael. "The world has to pay for my ruined life, do your worst; you have no power over hell."

"Read the old testament and you will see how much power Michael has over hell. I gave you a chance," Michael said, "more of a chance than you gave to any of your helpless victims so now it's time you met them all again."

With a wave of his hand the room filled with the spirits of Donald's victims and each one in turn aimed a devastating blow at the helpless murderer. He screamed again but this time it was a scream of physical agony rather than one of fright. As the blows rained down he began to lash out at his unseen tormentors. Suddenly the door of his bedroom was flung open just as Mrs Fairchild reached the landing. She saw Donald's contorted face as he knelt on his bed flailing his arms and screaming vile obscenities. She moved across the landing to the door but before she could enter the door slammed shut. Inside she could hear the din of a thousand voices cursing and screaming. She ran down the stairs and flung open the front door. Sergeant Knox was sitting in his car when he saw her dash out into the street and scream for help.

"Please somebody help me, Donald is being murdered, please help!"

Knox instinctively reached for his radio and called for back-up, he told the radio operator to get Draylock over there immediately, he didn't know what the hell was going on but he knew that Draylock would want to be the first to know whatever it was.

Knox leapt from the car and headed towards Mrs Fairchild.

"Oh please help me!" she gasped as she fell into his arms, "someone is trying to murder my son."

"Stay here and wait for the police," he said, then, he sprinted up the path to the front door. Inside the house he too heard the commotion coming from Donald's room and without thinking he ran towards it. He tried the door but it was locked solid. The noise from within the room sounded as if all of Bedlam had been let loose. He put the full weight of his shoulder to the door but still it wouldn't budge. "Open this door!" he demanded, "You can't get away, the police will be here in one minute."

His demands were as ineffectual as his shoulder and the door remained firmly closed. Soon the sound of sirens sped into the street and the screeching of tyres brought half a dozen police cars to a halt including that of Draylock and Davis. Within seconds they were in the house and racing up the stairs. "This is Chief Inspector Draylock Wiseman and if I were you I would open this door, I will count to three and then I will have it broken down." Knox hadn't noticed that the din in the room had started to subside the moment the sirens could be heard out in the street. The room was now quiet and as the words left Draylock's lips the door fell tamely open. Donald looked as though he was screaming but no sound came from his mouth; he was pulling his hair out by the roots. He looked at Draylock and began sobbing that he could see dead people.

"It sounds to me like it is time to settle this Donald, and give yourself some peace," Draylock said.

"They won't leave me alone. He told me that they will never leave me alone," he cried.

131

Donald dragged himself from the bed and moved slowly towards Draylock. Davis and Knox moved forward to protect him if Donald should be armed but Draylock motioned with his hand to let him come. With tears streaming down his face, Donald grabbed hold of Draylock's lapels. His eyes darted warily all over the room, "There are ghosts everywhere; can't you hear them? Can you not see them? They're beating me and laughing at me," he said.

"There is no one else here Donald, just us," Draylock said softly as he gently released Donald's hands from his coat. He could see that Donald was in a state of delusion.

"Please make them stop," he cried.

Draylock shook his head slowly: "Only you can do that Donald."

Putting his hands on Donald's shoulders, Draylock gently led Donald back to his bed and eased him slowly back down and sat beside him. Davis and Sergeant Knox stood at the open door and listened to the conversation. They sensed that Donald was about to break and it would have been inadmissible evidence if Draylock had listened to any confession inside a closed room.

Draylock calmly told Donald that he didn't have to say anything but if he did choose to it could be used in evidence against him. Donald shook his head: "I want to tell you; I have to tell you."

Draylock deftly motioned to Davis not to move any closer in case Donald decided to change tack again like he had done earlier back at the station; then he turned back to Donald,

"What have you done that makes you think you are being haunted?" he asked.

Looking at Draylock with glazed eyes Donald said: "Don't you know? They're dead because I killed them, all of them. I cut off their heads and hands and I did it all on my own."

"Who exactly did you kill Donald?" Draylock asked.

"I killed too many to remember," Donald said.

Draylock tried a different line of questioning: "OK then, how did you kill them Donald?"

The glazed expression on Donald's face seemed to clear instantly and he began to talk like an excited child, "I killed some of them with hammers and some of them with knives and the really weak ones I strangled," he said almost as if he was proud of his crimes.

Draylock looked briefly over to Davis before he carried on, "What did you do with the bodies after you killed them?"

"I cut off their heads and their hands," he said. He seemed to go almost into a daydream as he added with a whisper, "their beautiful hands."

"Donald, we know what you did with the heads but what did you do with the hands and the bodies?" Draylock said.

Donald was almost unaware of the question as he said: "They had beautiful hands you see, not like mine, I have butcher's hands. That's my trade you know. I was taught how to be a butcher by my father. I killed him too, you know." Then he turned his hands over for Draylock to look at. "See how ugly they are?"

Draylock looked at Donald's hands: "What did you do with all those beautiful hands Donald?"

133

"I saved them all," he said.

"Saved them all where?" Draylock asked.

"I can't tell you that because I'm keeping them." Donald said.

Draylock sensed that if he pushed him on the hands that he would loose him, so he moved on: "You said you killed your father Donald, why did you do that?"

Donald's eyes glazed over again and he became agitated, "Because he killed my mother when I was ten years old and I vowed I would kill him when I grew up, so I did. I avenged my mother's death. I'm not sorry for killing my father."

"And what did you do with his body?" Draylock asked.

"I cut his body up and put it through the mincing machine, then I made good use of it, he finally did something worthwhile," Donald smiled.

Draylock was puzzled: "How did you put it to good use?"

"I sold it as dog meat in my shop," Donald said. Then in the ensuing silence he went on to try to justify his actions: "Dogs are better than humans, they never let you down, they never get drunk, they never beat your mother and they stay loyal until they die, I'm glad I killed him and so are the dogs."

"And is that what you did with the other bodies Donald?" Draylock asked.

Donald bowed his head in a genuine show of remorse: "I know they didn't deserve to die, but they were beautiful and I am ugly, don't you see I had to kill all beauty to make my ugliness acceptable? I didn't want to destroy their bodies the same way as that bastard, but I had to, I wanted to stop and I tried to stop but after I killed him I couldn't stop killing I just had to keep on feeding the monster inside me."

Draylock had heard enough, the confession from Donald would be enough to convict him of the murders of all the young men found and an army of Elizabeth Ogylvies' would not be able to change the only possible outcome. There were still questions to be asked but they would have to wait until another time. Draylock beckoned Davis and Knox to have Wiseman taken to the station. They handcuffed him and led him down the stairs. In the hallway Mrs Fairchild looked pitifully at Donald and he stopped briefly.

"Was it you Donald who did all these horrible things?" she asked.

Donald didn't speak; he just hung his head and walked out to the waiting police van. Mrs Fairchild stopped Draylock and asked: "What will happen to him now?"

"That is up to other people to decide madam," he said softly.

"There is something which might help," she said.

"You have been helpful enough Mrs Fairchild; no one will hold you responsible for any of this," he said.

Mrs Fairchild held out the key to a heavy padlock and pointed back up the stairs,

"This is the key to the attic where Donald spent quite a lot of time, I have had arthritis for the past fifteen years and I have never been able to climb up there, but perhaps you should take a look."

Draylock turned to Davis, "Get forensics down here now," he said.

The forensics team found over thirty jars in the attic and in each jar there was a pair of preserved hands. At last the mystery of the Hamilton murders had been solved.

Wiseman was officially charged with multiple murder. He was sent on remand to a high security prison from where he would be taken to court. However, there was still one element of the case to be resolved, that of the involvement of the supernatural. Michael wanted Donald arrested and put in prison for murder but it seemed that other spirits wanted Donald dead. Each night in his cell, Donald would sit and wait for the laughter to start, it never did. Finally, Donald would put his head down to go to sleep. Only then would the laughter start, beginning quietly then steadily building until it reached such a high pitched screech that Donald would wake up screaming. The spirits attacked him every time he closed his eyes to sleep.

By the time Donald was taken to court, he was a nervous wreck. He did not even have the strength to stand up in court to give his name, and when he did he was continually looking around him as if he was looking for something or someone. The court hearing was adjourned for psychiatric reports and Donald was eventually pronounced unfit to stand trial. He was eventually incarcerated in a mental institution for the rest of his natural life.

Chapter 22

Donald had been in the institution almost a year when, one morning a nurse went to give him his medication and found his straight jacket in a heap on the floor. His wrists had been sliced open and he was hanging by his neck from the bars of his room with a sheet taken from his bed. A message written in blood on the wall simply said: "At last I will have some peace from Michael."

In all of the years that Draylock had spent on the force the hardest thing he ever had to do was to tell the parents of Michael Brewer that their son was dead. Their son would never return but at least they had the consolation of knowing that the man who murdered him was brought to justice in some way, they could also begin to grieve for their son unlike other parents who could never be certain if their sons had been the victims of Donald Wiseman.

Six months after the death of Donald Wiseman, it was decided to tear down the old abattoir where his grisly deeds had been carried out. It was thought that it would be a mark of respect for the families who had lost sons to the monster. Plans were proposed to turn the whole area into a lasting memorial to the dead and it was decided to build a proper playground for the village children in Shakleton's Clough; that would be a fitting tribute to the dead men and to the tragic life of Michael Brewer. Work began on demolishing the abattoir as soon as the plans were approved.

People from Hamilton and Chiswick joined local dignitaries gathered in the sunshine of an early June afternoon on the site of the newly completed memorial park and play area. The mayor of Chiswick unveiled a plaque set in a stone cairn, on the plaque were the names of all the young men whose names were to be immortalized by the memorial park. The mayor of Chiswick pulled the ceremonial cord as the mayor of Hamilton said these words: "Let this area not be only a memorial to our stolen loved ones, but let it be a symbol of the future and security of our youth hereafter."

The press cameras clicked and the film cameras rolled not only to spread the conclusion of the case to a waiting world but also to record the occasion for posterity. What the media did not record was the lone figure of Draylock as he walked back to his car, with his hands deep in his coat pockets. He had his retirement to look forward to and his crowning glory of such a distinguished police career was that of being credited with having solved one of the biggest crimes in local history, a crime which came to be known as the Wiseman murders. But you and I and of course Michael Brewer know who the real detective was.

The End

Printed in the United Kingdom
by Lightning Source UK Ltd.
131176UK00001B/8/P